P9-DWZ-374

Beverly Hills Prep

SHATTERED GLASS

SHANNON LAYNE

EPIC Escape

An Imprint of EPIC Press
abdopublishing.com

Shattered Glass
Beverly Hills Prep: Book #4

abdopublishing.com

Published by EPIC Press, a division of ABDO, PO Box 398166, Minneapolis, Minnesota 55439.

Printed in the United States of America, North Mankato, Minnesota.
052018
092018

Cover design by Laura Mitchell
Edited by Ryan Hume

Library of Congress Cataloging-in-Publication Data

Library of Congress Control Number: 2016962591

Publisher's Cataloging in Publication Data

Names: Layne, Shannon, author.
Title: Shattered glass/ by Shannon Layne
Description: Minneapolis, MN : EPIC Press, 2019 | Series: Beverly hills prep; #4
Summary: Victoria Cambridge is a senior at Beverly Hills Prep, and is getting tired of putting on the façade of being the mean ice princess. Her real interest is in mathematics, but her father has other plans. Can Victoria make him understand? Or will she have to turn away from her passion forever?
Identifiers: ISBN 9781680767117 (lib. bdg.) | ISBN 9781680767674 (ebook)
Subjects: LCSH: Role expectation--Fiction. | Parent-child relations--Fiction. | Private preparatory schools--Fiction. | Teenage girls--Fiction | Young adult fiction.
Classification: DDC [FIC]--dc23

For any girl brave enough to follow her heart.

I think my dream is pointing me
down another path.
—From the movie *Pocahontas* (1995)

Chapter One

Victoria Jane Cambridge woke up with her bare feet on her pillow, tugging her silk turquoise eye mask over her head as she wondered who was knocking on her door on a Saturday morning. She *hated* waking up early. She groped for her phone with one hand while shading her face from the sunlight entering through her lace curtains with the other hand. *What time is it?* She narrowed her ice blue eyes, shifted on her Egyptian-cotton bedspread, and grabbed her iPhone. It was about seven in the morning. There was another pounding at the door, and Victoria sighed. Of all the good habits that

Beverly Hills Prep had instilled in her, rising early was not one. If it were up to her, Victoria would happily sleep in until noon pretty much every day. And, as luck would have it, she'd forgotten to set an alarm for Saturday morning inspection. *This is just perfect.*

"Victoria? It's time for inspection. Are you there?"

"Aw man," muttered Victoria. Saturday morning inspection was the worst. It was just too early—*and who cleaned their room on the weekend, anyway?* Victoria glanced around her room, yanking back the curtains on her four-poster. She'd spent a year abroad and had become very attached to her English-style bed while in London. Wispy, pale blue material was yanked to the side and Victoria slid her feet into the plush of her white sheepskin rug. Her sheets were smooth white silk, the color of a glacier. Brushing her long hair back from her face, Victoria stood and gazed at her room, which was an unequivocal disaster. Another habit Beverly Hills

Prep was still trying to eradicate from her psyche: a tendency toward messiness. Inspection was just *not* going to work for her today.

Tugging on her sapphire satin robe, Victoria walked from her bedroom to the front door of her suite and opened it to a startled-looking prefect.

"Morning," said Victoria brightly. Thankfully, there was no dorm head accompanying her.

"Good morning, Victoria," said the prefect, some spindly girl Victoria knew from one of her classes. She was always getting her name wrong. *Cindy? Courtney?*

"It's time for room inspection," said the prefect. Victoria sighed and attempted a soulful expression.

"I'm afraid that's really not going to work for me today," she said, studying her nails. "I'm just not up for company at the moment."

"Room inspection isn't a party. It's a mandated requirement."

Victoria looked Prefect Cindy/Courtney straight

in the eyes, the smile fading from her rosebud lips. Her eyes could chill like a winter's night.

"Is it also a mandated requirement that you be really super annoying?"

The girl flushed; Victoria took advantage of the moment. She already had three strikes on her record from the previous semester, and it had been a pain to get the counselors to drop them. The last thing she needed was to start spring semester on the wrong foot.

"Please just give me a pass this one time," said Victoria. "Come on. You know I'm good for it. What will it take? Money, clothes? I've got both."

"Shut up," hissed the prefect. "Do you want someone to hear you?"

Victoria just gazed at her, then looked pointedly up and down the empty hallway. Even if someone was there, she knew no one was going to get her into trouble.

"There's no one to hear," said Victoria. "Or would you prefer something else? Do you have a secret ambition to be an actress? Looking for a summer internship?"

The prefect blushed again. Victoria watched the blotchy redness creep up her neck and felt vaguely nauseated. All she wanted was for this girl to leave so she could go back to bed. At least she was easy to manipulate. Everyone was, once you figured out what they wanted. And a lot of people at this school were interested in Victoria's father and what he had to offer. Not that Victoria blamed them—Richard Cambridge was the best in the business at what he did, and he didn't let anyone forget it. For as long as she could remember, Victoria had been watching her father dole out criticism harsh enough to make anyone from a lead actress to a chief financial officer cry on the spot. He was known as a hard man, with a temper that could be violent, and Victoria admitted it was true. She'd seen it many times. But she loved him. She had to—he was all she had.

Victoria's mother had left before Victoria turned five, a Swedish supermodel who had divorced her father after a tumultuous, brief marriage. She was Richard's second wife. He was on his fourth now, a photographer from Ireland with bright red hair and a loud laugh. Victoria was surprised to like Maureen much more than she had her father's third wife, but Maureen seemed too sweet for him. In all likelihood, Richard would end up alienating her with his rough personality and Maureen would leave like the others, so it was best not to get too attached. Victoria barely knew her own mother as it was. Lyra Wolffson was cold, not really the maternal type, and other than the checks she sent for Victoria's birthday (usually late), the contact they had was minimal. Not that Victoria cared. She had her dad, after all. Despite his multiple marriages, Richard had never had any other children. Victoria was all he had, and he showered her with attention and affection unlike any he showed his wives. Victoria loved him for that.

"I want to be a producer," said the prefect, and Victoria jolted back to the present. "I have a job at a company now, but if I could get in with some affiliate of Brightline somehow, even just something unpaid—"

"Yeah, I'll see what I can do," said Victoria. Just listening to the girl was making her head pound. "It's no problem, um, Clarissa. I'll talk to my father." She wouldn't, but this girl didn't need to know that.

"It's Clara."

"Right, sorry."

Victoria flashed one of her thousand-watt smiles and stepped slowly back into her room. "So, are we good here? I'll talk to my father and get back to you on that, and you just give me full points on my room inspection?"

"You're lucky the dorm head isn't with me today," grumbled Clara, "but yes, fine."

"You're a doll," said Victoria. "Thank you so much." She shut the door gently.

Chapter Two

Victoria walked back into her bedroom and flopped onto the bed, sending up a few feathers from her down comforter. While dealing with that silly prefect had definitely given her a headache, it wasn't the first time that being the only child of Richard Cambridge had been an advantage.

As the heiress to the entirety of Brightline Productions, Victoria was the child of a man who had made his fortune in the entertainment industry to an unprecedented level. More than half of all major motion pictures produced here and internationally were either direct products of the company, or at least products of affiliates that had been bought out by Brightline.

Victoria had grown up with people like Steven Spielberg at her birthday parties; she'd been in small onscreen roles since she was two months old, playing an infant in one of her father's movies. As she got older, though, she started to earn her parts. Practically being raised on movie sets, from Los Angeles to Bangkok to Madrid, meant that Victoria was comfortable on set in a way that few children were.

She had grown up traveling with her father, either on trips representing the company's business interests or to the sets themselves, and that familiarity bred confidence. Victoria would never be shy in front of a camera, and her father encouraged her to act. He became even more passionate about it than Victoria was herself, bursting with pride when she effortlessly memorized lines, or delivered a scene flawlessly. Acting was easy, natural, but not something she was necessarily dedicated to. Instead, she became more interested in the behind-the-scenes creation of the film and the way that sets were engineered. Something about watching the creation of another world, the angle of the shots and the way that things were formatted and built became much more interesting. Not that she really knew how to explain that to her dad. She also didn't know how to explain to him that she'd applied to a couple of technical colleges this fall. As far as Richard was concerned, Victoria would graduate from Beverly Hills Prep and jump right into the family business—as an actress. And Victoria just wasn't sure that was what she wanted.

As Victoria lay there, thinking it all through, her phone started to ring. She sighed, reaching for it, already knowing it would be her dad.

"Hey, Dad."

"Hi, kiddo. How's it going?"

"Good, everything is good."

"Plans for the weekend?"

"Nothing crazy. I think I'm supposed to hang out with Annabelle at some point today."

If she isn't still mad about last night. Well, whatever, thought Victoria. She used to like Annabelle because she was just a little mean and that was amusing to her. Now, Annabelle's attitude was more grating, but they'd been friends for long enough that she was hard to shrug off.

"Good, good. Want to grab lunch?"

"Today? Wait, I thought you were still in Taiwan."

He'd been on another business trip. Her father spent so much time traveling that Victoria honestly didn't try to keep up with where he was when he was abroad. It was just too much work.

"I got back early. I'm staying at the house here in Beverly Hills."

"Oh, great. Well yeah, I'm basically free today."

"Great. Can I pick you up in an hour, sweetie?"

"Sounds good, Daddy."

Victoria hung up and flipped over on her bed.

Sliding off the silky sheets, she walked across piles of clothes toward the bathroom. It was chaos, but it was a chaos she enjoyed. The newest tops she'd gotten on her shopping trip over Christmas break were the ones all piled into the corner across from her bed. Tags from Chanel, Versace, Givenchy, and Armani littered the floor and swung from the pieces they were still attached to.

The fact that she had to wear a uniform every single day at this school was a constant source of agitation to Victoria. She had enough clothes to fill six closets and she could only bring a third of it to school, and she hardly got to wear what she had as it was. It wasn't that she didn't look good in the uniform—she definitely did—it was just that she looked better in Dolce & Gabbana. Well, for today at least, she could wear something besides plaid or a button-up shirt to breakfast with her dad.

Victoria's hair flowed down her back like ocean waves, drying in soft curls like it always did. She enjoyed her curls, the way that she enjoyed the scent of the sea, or the rush of happiness she felt when she saw her father—all familiar things that she found comfort in. Richard Cambridge picked up his daughter in the usual black SUV, whose various models and makes (always brand new) she'd become used to in her eighteen years, and Victoria hugged him as she got into the car. He smelled like cigars and cologne.

"Hey, Dad," said Victoria. "How was your trip?"

"Deathly dull. I left as soon as I could, once the meetings were finished."

"Is the new movie a go?"

"Of course. We just signed the contracts. I got James Cameron to direct like I wanted, and the extra budget room we need."

"James is directing? Good." Victoria's favorite movie genres were sci-fi or fantasy—she was obsessed with special effects and the way that teams could take something of this world and make it look like something completely different onscreen.

"Isn't it? He's perfect for this project."

The talk about movies and the nitty gritty details of a production was second nature to them both. They were still discussing when they arrived at the restaurant, a tiny place suited for lunch that was Victoria's favorite. They were escorted inside by Richard's ever-present bodyguards as the driver parked, and Victoria smiled at the hostess as they went in and were immediately seated, despite the line around the block. It was a perk she'd gotten used to over the years, due to her family name. She didn't think she'd be totally snobby if the courtesy wasn't extended to her for some reason, but it would definitely be unsettling, and a little annoying not to have that extra attention lavished on her.

Victoria wasn't ashamed to admit that she liked luxury, having grown up with it. But, she also didn't need it the way some of her classmates did, ones who had lived similarly privileged lives. Movie sets weren't always in Positano, or South Africa. She'd spent a month in a village on Madagascar, weeks on sweltering South Pacific islands eating nothing but rice and enduring peeling skin from the burning sun. Sure, she was always going to be privileged, and she knew it, but that didn't mean she was a spoiled brat. At least not all the time.

"So, since we're talking about the new project," said her father after they'd ordered, "I'd like you to come in for an audition for a supporting role after you graduate this spring. Get your feet wet in something with a bigger budget."

Even as the daughter of someone like Richard Cambridge, Victoria auditioned for parts. Though her chances were exponentially greater than an unknown actress, her father's influence was best used for landing her auditions and readings. Then both she and the director got a chance to see the role and how it would fit her.

There had been times where she'd read for a role she thought she'd be perfect for, only to say the lines aloud and realize it wasn't the right fit. Plus, Victoria didn't want to take jobs based purely on her father's influence. She had the satisfaction of knowing that while she was lucky to have been born into the family name she had, she was still a viable talent in her own right.

Victoria toyed with the straw in her hot chocolate. She did want to be a part of the new movie—she could learn a lot with James at the helm. But she didn't want to act in it. The more that she got into her math and physics classes, the more she was toying with the idea of going to a school known for science, and a good one. She'd applied to several of those schools, just in case, on a whim. If she changed her mind, she reasoned, then she just wouldn't go.

She'd filled out an application for MIT, and one for Caltech, and promptly forgot about them, or pushed them from her mind. But now that spring was coming, those letters back from schools would be coming in. And Victoria wasn't sure which she'd be more relieved to see—an acceptance or a denial. In many ways, a denial would probably be easier.

"So, when I graduate, you really just want me to go to college online?" said Victoria.

"We can work it out that way, yeah," said her dad, in his typical gruff, straightforward fashion. "I didn't get a degree until I'd started my first company, you know that. Sure, I have my MBA now, but I didn't get it until I was in my thirties. I just think you're better off getting some further real life experience as soon as you can."

"Yeah, sure," said Victoria. "I just, I don't know Dad. I kind of thought I might do something a little different."

"Like an indie film? There are a couple really viable ones that have come my way lately that you'd be perfect for, Tori. When you get the scripts we can read through them together. You're talented, honey. You're right. Let's look at all your options before we decide for sure."

As her dad started going into the logistics of

her working on set that summer, Victoria sighed. She heard the pride in his voice, and she loved him for that. The waitress brought their orders over. Victoria picked at her eggs Benedict while her dad started in on the biggest omelet she'd ever seen. Victoria chewed her lip, unsure what to say. She couldn't tell him she wasn't sure a future in front of the camera was what she wanted. She definitely couldn't tell him about the colleges she'd applied to. What would he say? The look on his face would be too much to bear. And he was all she had. Her dad had always been the constant in her life. What if she lost him, too?

Chapter Three

Victoria remembered the days when she would've spent all of Sunday lying on the grass of the campus quad, bored and gossiping about every girl in the school. Now, she spent most of it studying in her room like a nerd.

How had this happened?

It had been so gradual that she hadn't really noticed for a long time. The first two years at Beverly Hills Prep had been a blur of doing pretty much nothing, skating by in her classes, and generally just messing around. She was still acting a lot, so she was gone much of the time for those parts.

Her grades had slipped in her math classes most of all, and then Mrs. Gable had entered the picture.

Mrs. Gable had dark hair and a booming laugh, and she was one of the youngest teachers in the school, as well as a student body favorite. While her sense of humor made classes fun and interesting, she also didn't let her students get away with anything. The woman had worked at NASA before coming to Beverly Hills Prep, and she had a mind like a nuclear physicist. Her math classes were the hardest ones in the entire school. She was the only teacher Victoria had been unable to get around with her usual methods of charm and whining.

Instead, when her grades dipped, Mrs. Gable forced her to come in for tutoring sessions. It was only during the course of those sessions that both Mrs. Gable and Victoria herself realized she had a knack for numbers. Physics was what really spoke to Victoria—she could actually visualize the problems, the way things would fit together. No teacher had ever pushed her to discover that before, not in her whole life, until Mrs. Gable.

So, today, instead of painting her nails in Annabelle's room, or gossiping on the quad, or organizing a shopping excursion in Beverly Hills, Victoria was solving a series of calculus proofs for Mrs. Gable. They'd been working through a couple of them last week, and Victoria had promised to finish the ones they'd been stuck on for the Math Mania team that Mrs. Gable headed.

Victoria had been helping the team out for a while now, too, on terms of complete secrecy. Just because she liked math didn't mean she wanted to completely jeopardize her social standing by joining a team as nerdy as Math Mania. She was Victoria Cambridge, for goodness' sake. If the whole school found out about her geeky tendencies, even she would never be able to live it down. Better to just get through her senior year without having to deal with that drama.

Sighing, Victoria shut her Calculus book and

rubbed her tired eyes. Checking her phone, she answered a text from her dad confirming that she was free for dinner on Saturday night; when he was in the area, they met up as often as he was available, since he was away so often. Yawning, Victoria decided it was definitely time to call it a night. She had a standing after-school appointment with Mrs. Gable tomorrow, and she'd better be rested or she'd never be able to keep up. She was taking Mrs. Gable's Advanced Calculus class as well as Honors Physics.

On top of that, she'd promised the teacher to come in early to help with a lesson plan for her first period Geometry class. In reality, Victoria thought the teacher was hiding something from her. She'd never asked Victoria to come in early before—their sessions were strictly after school. Whatever she wanted, Victoria had a sense she wasn't going to like it. But what choice did she have? The woman hadn't failed her in her second year even though she'd definitely deserved it. *Looks like this Monday morning will be an early one,* Victoria thought.

Sure enough, Victoria's alarm on Monday morning was violent, earsplitting, and unwelcome. Why, why had Mrs. Gable wanted to see her so early? The sun wasn't even up yet. This was like a medieval torture method. Victoria tugged her uniform over her head and zipped her skirt with her eyes closed. Groping for her shoes, she slipped on her favorite flats and then swept her hair into a messy ponytail that was casual, but still adorable. Her backpack was packed and waiting by the door, and Victoria grabbed it on her way out, still muttering about evil teachers.

Mrs. Gable's classroom was all the way in the back of the new Koroleva Mathematics building. The flooring, lights, and doors were all brand new and completely redone. It felt familiar and welcome to Victoria, probably due to all the time she'd spent here in the past year. She knocked on Mrs. Gable's door and then let herself in. The classroom was empty except for the teacher herself, seated at the desk in the front of the classroom. There were both whiteboards and a SMART board for teaching purposes, and a state-of-the-art projection system built into the ceiling that Victoria had actually helped the maintenance staff install one afternoon.

Mrs. Gable looked up from her lesson plan as Victoria entered, her dark hair pulled back into a severe bun.

"Good morning, Victoria," she said, sipping coffee from a mug decorated with the Pythagorean Theorem that said, "Math Rules!"

"Is it?" said Victoria sourly. She dropped her backpack on the floor and tugged a chair up to the desk. "What do you need my help with? It's too early for math."

"It's never too early for math," chuckled Mrs. Gable. "But I am sorry to ask you to come in so early."

She stirred her coffee as Victoria yawned.

"There is something I'd like to ask you, though," said Mrs. Gable. "Something I think we need to speak frankly about."

"It really can't wait until I'm a little more awake?" Victoria yawned, but she saw Mrs. Gable's expression was serious. "Alright, alright, I'm sorry. What do you want to discuss?"

"You've been helping me out with Math Mania for a while now. Since your sophomore or junior year, if I recall correctly."

"Yeah, I guess. Just as another incentive for you to bring my grades up, really."

"Sure. But still. You've been around the team a lot. You know the way the competitions work, how to come up with a solution under pressure."

Victoria nodded suspiciously.

"Look, Sara's become really sick. She had appendicitis and went into surgery early this morning."

Sara was a second-year student on the Math

Mania team, with dark hair and a shy smile. Victoria's brow furrowed with concern.

"Wow, that's awful. Is she going to be okay?"

"Yeah, she should be fine, but she'll be out this entire week. And we have a competition in Riverside next Friday."

"Can't Lucille fill in?"

"Her study abroad semester began last week, and even if she were here, I wouldn't want her filling in since she was originally an alternate. There's someone else I have in mind."

"Who?"

Mrs. Gable just stared at Victoria, sipping coffee out of her mug and blinking innocently. Realization dawned on Victoria, and she shook her head.

"No. Come on. No way."

"Victoria, please. Just this one time. It's the last competition of the year."

"What about state finals? That's after the regional semifinals."

"In all likelihood we won't make it to state, so

don't worry about that. There's no way we'll win the semi-finals, and that's fine. I just want the team to be able to compete."

"I've never competed with the team before!"

"I know. I can write you in as a stand-in team member due to a medical emergency."

"I don't know about this, Mrs. Gable. I don't mind helping out the team, and you've been a big help with those college applications and everything else, but this is too much."

"There could be important people at the event, Victoria. Admissions officers, for one, looking for STEM majors and other candidates worth pursuing."

"Look, I never even said I was interested in all that. I appreciated you bringing me the applications for MIT and the California Institute of Technology, but I really just filled those out as a last resort type of thing. I only applied to two places—like, I don't think my chances are great. I mean, my dad wants me to be in a movie this summer. I don't know that

I'd go to either of those places even on the very slim chance that I did get in." Victoria wasn't trying to sound mean, she really wasn't, but the idea of actually being on the Math Mania team was just too much to deal with.

"I understand that, I really do, but we really need you for this spot. I don't expect to win, by any means, but like I said, it's the team's last chance to compete for the year and I don't want them all to have to forfeit that on a technicality."

Victoria had been working closely enough with Mrs. Gable for long enough to know that the Math Mania put forth a lot of effort, but didn't necessarily perform too well in competitions. The kids that were on it were smart, but often got stage fright and didn't do well under the pressure of an event. Under Mrs. Gable's direction, though, the team had started to rise through the ranks. Not that Victoria was paying attention to something that geeky, or anything.

"Isn't there someone else who could fill in?"

"No one who I would trust to not totally mess up on such short notice. Look, I don't want to browbeat you into this, okay? I just thought you'd be a good fit and figured I'd ask. If you change your mind in the next day or so, let me know, and I'll add you to the list. If not, that's okay. I wanted to extend the invitation."

Victoria tapped on the desk, her chin in her hand. She stood by her words—she was not at all sure she wanted to participate in this thing, but she did feel a twinge of guilt, and just a little curiosity.

"Do you really think I could do it?"

"I really do. You've come a long way since you were failing my math class, largely due to laziness rather than an inability to do the work."

"Thanks."

"It's the truth. You're my best Physics student. And I know that isn't just because of the time you spend on your homework."

"What do you mean?"

"You have an actual talent for this. Untapped, largely, and I'd like to see it developed."

"Do you really think so?"

"I do. As I said, you've come a long way in a short time. I think you could go as far in this realm, so to speak, as you wanted."

Victoria looked at her teacher. Mrs. Gable was smiling, and Victoria smiled hesitantly back. Her head was spinning.

"Thanks," said Victoria, slowly. "I appreciate all that, a lot. Um, let me think about the whole Math Mania thing, okay? I still don't think it's my thing, but I'll keep it in mind."

"That's fine. I understand."

"Thank you," said Victoria, her mind spinning.

Mrs. Gable smiled at her.

"Now, do you actually want to help me out by grading a few of these Geometry tests, since you're here?"

"Sure," said Victoria, and she took the red pen and let her mind go quiet as she flipped through the pages. She had a lot to think about, and she wasn't sure she was ready to tackle it all.

Chapter Four

That evening, the dining hall served glazed roast duck with pepper and spices, a goat cheese fennel salad, and a triple-layer chocolate mousse cake for dessert. Victoria's friends served a healthy dose of pointless gossip.

"There's no way those purses she's always carrying around are the real designers," Lulu was saying.

"No, I really think they are," Annabelle disagreed. "I'm not sure how she can afford them, but they're the real thing. Didn't you see Bethany carrying a brand new Louis Vuitton just yesterday? She said her father brought it back for her from France, but they're only selling that style in the states. And Bethany's father just declared bankruptcy—there's no way she could afford it, but she has it. I think Margot has something to do with it for sure. I just don't know what."

Victoria noted that Annabelle seemed to have gotten over the fact that the group had gone to that party without her. No one was willing to listen to her complain about it anymore at least, so she'd given it up. *Thank goodness.*

Victoria poked at her food, leaning her head on her other hand and tuning out the chatter. What was wrong with her? She used to enjoy the idle gossip a lot more than she did now. It had been her bread and butter. Today was just a hard day to listen to her friends talk about things she didn't care about when she had so much on her mind.

"Victoria? Victoria? Hello, Earth to you." Annabelle poked her in the side, and Victoria jumped just a little before narrowing her eyes at Annabelle. She hated being surprised.

"Sorry, what?"

"We were just asking if you knew anything about the whole purse scenario. It just seems like a lot of girls have designers they can't afford."

"Oh, right. I don't really care," said Victoria, yawning. Annabelle gritted her teeth, and the rest of the girls tittered, but Victoria didn't care if Annabelle was offended. It fit her reputation, anyway—she was thought of as an ice princess-type already, so being mean sometimes just kept her reputation intact. Maybe it was stupid to want to keep her reputation as being just a little unapproachable, but Victoria sort of liked it that way. It made it seem like girls were in awe of her, just a little. Of course, being in movies helped with that too.

"I'm going to go work out before Study Hall," said Victoria.

"What, why? You already have the perfect body," said Lulu, a freshman on the dance team. Victoria rewarded her with a smile, and Annabelle scowled.

"You're sweet. I'll see you guys later. Remember, study group in my suite tonight."

She got up and left the dining hall, leaving her tray where it was. Back in her room, she tugged on yoga pants and a loose shirt, enjoying the feeling of taking her uniform off. She tossed her skirt and top on the floor with the rest of her clothes and made a mental note to tell the laundry staff to take care of it. On top of her private suite, one of the only ones available on campus, Victoria also had a laundry service and a concierge on call. Unfortunately, her laundry service was Mondays and she never remembered to tell her dad that she needed to switch it, so despite all the assistance, come Saturday inspection her room was still more likely to be a mess than neat and tidy. It was so annoying. Plugging her headphones into her ears, Victoria headed for the workout center, ready to spend some time on a treadmill and think about everything Mrs. Gable had said to her.

After an hour on the treadmill, Victoria's legs were shaky and her chest felt like it was on fire. She stepped off, wiping at her brow with a towel, and headed for the locker room. Since she hated showering off in the locker rooms, where other people's sweaty feet had been, she just grabbed her gym bag and swung it over her shoulder, earbuds still pumping Metallica. Loud, blasting music was what she preferred when she worked out, and she left it at a high volume as she left the workout center and started across campus back to her dorm.

The sun was just starting to set, and the sky over the quad was pink and orange, the color of a child's frozen treat. She would admit that the Beverly Hills Prep campus was one of the most beautiful she'd ever been on. She remembered when she'd first come here. She'd felt like she would trade it in a second for something with a little more variety.

Her boarding school in Barcelona, for one, had a campus that practically shared a street with a market that was always bustling and full of people waiting to sell beautiful linen clothes made from pure white cotton, or dancing skirts full of rich color. Victoria loved Los Angeles, the chaos and the endless lights, but this wasn't Los Angeles. After a while, though, Victoria had grown to appreciate campus for what it was. It was strange to think it was her last year here.

There was a lot she wouldn't miss, like being stuck with so many girls every hour of every day, but she'd miss some things—the sunsets, for one. The libraries. The food wasn't half bad, either. And Mrs. Gable. One of the very first people who hadn't been at all dazzled by her name or her relative fame and had instead pushed her in a way no one else ever had, except maybe her dad. He believed in her too, Victoria was sure of that, but he believed in her ability to act. She wasn't sure that confidence extended to physics and calculus, or if he even cared about those realms at all, even if she did.

"Victoria? Honey?"

Victoria turned to the woman tapping her shoulder as she pulled out one of her headphones.

"Yes, Miss Lorna?"

The woman had to be ninety years old, and she was almost always the receptionist, or dorm head on duty in the evenings. She was sweet, though, and always wearing adorable little pantsuits or dresses in shades of peach and mint.

"It's nearly time for Study Hall check-in. You should get to your room now, dear. You don't want a check on your record so soon into spring semester, do you?"

"No, ma'am. I'll go now."

She felt a little ridiculous talking to the lady as though she were some sort of Southern belle—*ma'am*? She'd never called anyone that in her life until she met Miss Lorna. The woman just brought it out in her.

Victoria walked down the hallway toward her suite, putting her earbud back in as she went. She took a deep breath, letting the exertion of her workout calm her. Her dad always said the best way to clear your mind for a new part was to go for a run, and Victoria stood by that advice. Her mind felt clearer, but she still wasn't sure what she was going to do about the Math Mania competition. It was silly to think of going to compete, really. She was a senior, and her college applications were already sent in. She couldn't very well use this as an excuse to pad the extracurricular section.

Victoria unlocked the door to her suite and sailed in, shutting it gently behind her. If she hurried, there would be enough time to shower before Study Hall officially began. The hot water soothed her nerves and relaxed her, and Victoria tugged on the lush cashmere sweatshirt and pants combo that Beverly Hills Prep sold in the student store (for those who could afford it, of course.) The crest and motto of the school were emblazoned on the front of the sweatshirt, and the set was conveniently approved for casual dress days and Study Hall.

A knock came at the door and Victoria opened it to Clara the prefect again.

"Study Hall check-in," piped Clara. "You can stay in your room or go to a library, but electronics are prohibited."

"I'm staying in my room tonight. I'm hosting a study meeting for my friends here."

"Do they all have signed passes approving group study?"

Victoria resisted the urge to roll her eyes. Barely.

"Yes, of course."

"Alright then. I'll need those passes at the end of Study Hall."

Victoria opened her mouth to snap at her, but Clara was already scurrying off to boss someone else around. Shutting the door again, Victoria quickly surveyed the sitting room area of her suite. It was spotless, thanks to the cleaning service, and a fire had been lit in the brick fireplace. Victoria took a seat on the chintz vintage sofa, which was a dark rosebud that perfectly set off the gold edging of the

Beverly Hills Prep crest that was mounted on the far wall, and the genuine Velázquez painting that hung next to the fireplace. Used to luxurious furnishings, Victoria felt right at home with the décor. She tugged over her lap a soft, genuine fur blanket, also bearing Beverly Hills Prep insignia, as her friends came in the door.

Chapter Five

"Have you guys done the reading for Poetry yet?" asked Annabelle an hour later, curled on Victoria's couch. "There's, like, forty pages of it."

"Of poetry? How is that even possible?" said Lulu.

"Mrs. Riley is crazy. She wants us to read basically all poetry ever written."

"I finished yesterday," said Victoria, who was in the middle of trying to solve a Physics proof. She always got her reading done for her classes that didn't involve math early in the week so she'd have more time to focus on Calculus and Physics.

All she needed to do was pass in those non-math classes, anyway, not excel. If she didn't get a perfect grade in Poetry, that was just fine. But she cared, for whatever reason, about her math classes. Maybe because she knew she could excel, or because Mrs. Gable had encouraged her for so long.

"Mrs. Gable gives out so much homework in Geometry," complained Lulu. "I'm never going to finish."

"I can help you with it if you want," said Victoria. "It's easy."

"Since when are you a math genius?" said Annabelle.

"That would be great actually," Lulu said with relief. "I don't get this stuff at all."

"Speaking of Mrs. Gable," said Vivi, "how come you're always in her classroom? Didn't you finish your required tutoring with her, like, forever ago?"

The question was asked politely, but it still caught Victoria off guard. Vivi had been quiet around the group for the first half of the year and was just now starting to return to her sassy self. Victoria chewed her lip as she quickly debated how much to share with the group.

"Yeah, but she gave me a bunch of options to do for extra credit, and I figured it couldn't hurt to pad my grade a little," said Victoria. "So, I've been helping her out, you know, when I have the time."

"That's nice of you," said Vivi.

"Yeah it is," said Annabelle, her eyes narrowing slightly. "Especially since your grades don't even matter anyway, and definitely not at this point. My mom heard that you're going to be in that James Cameron movie shooting this summer that your father is producing."

Lulu squealed; Vivi raised her eyebrows but didn't say anything. Lulu's roommate, who Victoria had literally just realized was also in the room, just sort of sat there looking either dumbstruck or just dazed from hunger. It was hard to say, but Victoria had definitely noticed the girl dropping weight. She was starting to look like a skeleton.

"Nothing is for sure yet," said Victoria. "I don't know which parts are available, and I'd still have to read for them. I haven't even seen a script yet. And deadlines change for movies all the time. Nothing is set in stone."

"That is just the coolest," gushed Lulu. "To get to be in a movie. I'm so jealous."

"Don't go talking about it to everyone," said Victoria, with a pointed glare at Annabelle. "It's still under negotiation and I can't really talk about it because it's one of my dad's projects."

"We won't say anything, relax," said Annabelle. "But seriously, why are you wasting your time after school with Mrs. Gable? It's just math class. I think it's weird."

"Not that it's really any of your business, but I like her," said Victoria, irritated. "And I'm good at math so it's not like it's hard to help out."

"Just so long as you don't do anything like join that stupid Math Mania team," snorted Annabelle, and Lulu giggled. "Oh my gosh—could you imagine? Every single girl on that team is such a geek."

"You're on the dance team," said Victoria, slamming her book shut. "So is Lulu. Viv is on the gymnastics team. How is Math Mania any different?"

The girls all stared at Victoria for a few seconds. She sat back against the couch and tried to act casual. Where had that outburst come from? What did she care if they thought Math Mania was geeky?

"I don't know, it's just an academic team, you know," said Annabelle after another moment had passed. "It's different."

"I guess," said Victoria, trying to act as though she didn't really care much either way.

"Can you read through this poetry with me, Annabelle?" said Vivi. "I don't get these last three lines."

"Ugh, yeah, Poe is really hard," said Annabelle, and the tension in the room was broken. Victoria went back to her problem, trying to act aloof, as though she wasn't affected by the conversation. Well, she hadn't known that she'd leap to the defense of Math Mania that way, to be fair. What was the matter with her? She thought it was a geeky club just like Annabelle did. So, what was the big deal? Why did it make her so mad when other people made those comments?

Because she actually knew Mrs. Gable, maybe, and she knew how much the club meant to the teacher. Maybe because somehow, all these weeks of helping out had made it matter to her, too. And maybe, just a little bit, she wanted to do it almost as a test for herself. Just to see if she could. If she totally froze up and fell on her face, well, she could just never do it again and act like it had never happened. But if she did well, as Mrs. Gable seemed to think she could, then she'd know if this part of her life was even worth pursuing at all.

Victoria went back to her homework, her pencil tracing numbers idly in the margins as she considered her options.

"Can you help me out with this problem, Victoria?" asked Lulu, breaking through her distraction. "If you don't mind. I'm having a really hard time with this one."

"Oh, yeah. Sure thing," said Victoria, scooting closer to Lulu on the couch and checking the problem in her textbook. "Let's see. Yeah, I can see from your work that you're on the right track, you just got stuck on the equation."

"Yeah. I plugged in all the numbers where it says to, but I'm still not getting the right answer when I check in the back of the book."

"It's this section right here," said Victoria, pointing in the text for Lulu. "You're missing a step on this calculation and it's messing up the equation. Try it this way instead."

She sketched out the problem for Lulu, showing her where she'd missed a part of the equation. Victoria helped Lulu type it correctly into her calculator, and then sat back as Lulu did the last part of the problem on her own.

"I got it!" said Lulu, checking her answer in the back of the book again. "Thanks, Victoria. I finally figured out what I was doing wrong. You're the best."

"No problem," said Victoria, laughing. "I barely helped you at all. You did most of it on your own."

As everyone went back to studying, Victoria chewed on her pencil and sighed. If the conversation before hadn't sealed her decision, then helping Lulu had. She needed to find Mrs. Gable tomorrow morning, first thing, to see if there was still time to tell her she'd changed her mind.

Chapter Six

Victoria was up so early the next morning that she had time to break in the French espresso machine that had been hooked up in the sitting room for the past year, at least. Clutching her thermos of cappuccino, Victoria walked briskly across campus as the sun came up, determined to catch Mrs. Gable before her first early class of the day. The more she'd begun to consider agreeing to participate in the competition, the more excited she'd gotten about it. Maybe that excitement was mixed with a lot of nerves and a healthy dose of pure fear, but that was normal, right?

Victoria knocked on Mrs. Gable's door, then went ahead and opened it before the teacher had a chance to say anything.

"Victoria," said Mrs. Gable, sitting at her desk. "Yes, please come in. Nice to see you so early. Did we have an appointment?"

"No, we didn't," said Victoria. "Sorry to burst in on you like this, but I wanted to tell you something."

"Yes?"

"I changed my mind. I want to compete with the Math Mania team at the semifinals."

The words came out in a rush, and Victoria wanted to wince at how geeky they sounded, but she held her ground. Mrs. Gable tapped a pencil on her lesson plans, studying Victoria carefully.

"Are you sure, Victoria? This is something you'll need to commit to. You can't just tell me now that you'll do it and then drop back out again. Semifinals are a week from Friday. That's barely enough time to have you come in and work with the team a few times before we go to the competition, so I don't want any more switch ups at this late hour."

"You're the one who asked me to compete," said Victoria, a little testily. "And I said I would. I'm not just going to flake out on you."

Mrs. Gable tapped her pencil a few more times, and then she smiled.

"Alright, then. I'm really glad you said yes, Victoria."

"Could've fooled me," said Victoria. "For a second there I thought you sounded disappointed."

Mrs. Gable laughed out loud, leaning back in her chair.

"I'm sorry. No, I'm definitely not disappointed. I just wanted to make sure you'd thought this through before I got excited about having you compete. You'll need to have a parent sign off on your attendance at the event, as well as a pass allowing you to leave campus."

"That's fine," said Victoria. She'd thought about

that part, too. If she chickened out and didn't feel brave enough to tell her dad what she was really doing, she could always lie and say it was just a field trip or something. He wouldn't care; he'd been signing most of her forms without looking at them since the third grade. Or, more often, if he was away on business, his assistant would copy it for her and fax the forms back to Victoria. Since Victoria was supposed to have dinner with him this week, though, it looked like she would need to ask him in person. It would look too suspicious if she asked his assistant to fax them over when he was available, and she didn't want to irritate him in case she decided to tell him what she was actually doing at the event. The better his mood was, the more likely that he would hear her out and not just demand that she start focusing on her career after high school and stop wasting her time in clubs that couldn't help her succeed in the business he loved.

"Okay, then," said Mrs. Gable. "Come to Math Mania practices this week and we'll make sure you're prepared to compete with the team next weekend. Here are those permission slips—get those signed and back to me as soon as possible."

"Is next week okay? I have dinner with my dad this weekend, and I can ask him then."

"That should be fine."

Victoria took a deep breath, clutching the paperwork in her hands. Then she straightened her shoulders and lifted her chin; she was Victoria Cambridge, after all. There was no reason to be nervous or afraid.

Mrs. Gable smiled at her, and Victoria smiled back.

"Thanks, Mrs. Gable. I won't let you down."

"I never doubted it," said Mrs. Gable, and Victoria left the classroom, letting the door close gently behind her.

The next few days absolutely flew by for Victoria.

There was a blur of Math Mania practices, along with all the other homework in her other classes, and on top of that, she was still trying to act normal around her friends. That in and of itself was no easy task, considering that Victoria was spending most of her free time testing her mathematics speed skills, which was definitely not typical Victoria behavior. The way that the competition worked was that there were two teams competing at a time, and a judge would project questions up on a board and the team to answer first won a certain number of points. As the rounds progressed, the questions became more complex and difficult to solve. There would be a total of three questions per round, and there were ten rounds in a match. Whichever team had the most points at the end of the final round was declared the victor. Five competitors for each team were allowed on the floor at all times, and now one of those five would be Victoria. She already knew she wasn't expected to answer every question by any means—she was brand new and had just begun to practice with the team in earnest, but she still wanted to be able to contribute. If she could be the fastest team member to just one question, even, that would be enough for her. But answering math questions correctly under that kind of pressure was harder than Victoria had truly understood until now. It would be totally different up on stage with an actual judge and not just Mrs. Gable at her desk presenting the problems.

"Earth to Victoria. Why are you staring at that math book like it has the secret to eternal youth inside?" said Annabelle. Victoria quickly shut the Calculus book she'd been studying at the table in the dining hall and sneered at her.

"Nope, just the secret to everlasting friendship. It involves not sticking your nose into other people's business quite so often."

Annabelle's cheeks turned a mottled red, and Victoria sighed and took another bite of her caramel-glazed crème brûlée, even though it had gone cold in the time she'd been looking at her book.

Lulu's roommate—her name was Marina, Victoria had finally realized—was staring at it longingly.

"I just have a ton of big tests coming up," said Victoria. "And I'm trying not to, like, fail them at least."

"Speaking of which, I actually failed that test we had on Monday," Lulu chimed in. "So, like, I could probably use a little of Victoria's focus."

"If you would just do any of your homework you wouldn't fail," snapped Annabelle, and Victoria licked the last bit of crème brûlée from her fork and got up to leave the table.

"Gym, then bed," she said, and waved to the girls as she left the dining hall. In reality, she was just heading back to her room so she could keep studying in peace. At least it was finally Friday, so she could use the entire weekend to continue preparing for the competition. Only one week to go until it was time.

As Victoria walked down the hallway toward her suite, her phone vibrated in her pocket. It was her dad, confirming that he'd send a car to pick her up the following night for dinner. Victoria texted him back, then blew out an anxious breath. *What if he won't sign my forms?* It seemed unlikely, but possible. He and Victoria had never really had anything to fight over before. They'd always been on the same page when it came to, well, everything, until now. What if he treated her the way she'd seen him treat his ex-wives during a divorce—including her mom? Victoria bit her lip. *He would never do that,* she told herself. *I'm just being stupid.*

Chapter Seven

The next evening, despite the fact that she'd just confirmed with him the night before, Victoria completely forgot that she had dinner plans with her father. She was reminded by her cell phone buzzing as she worked her way through a particularly thorny Calculus proof. It seemed as though she'd been studying for years at this point, but she couldn't stop. Her nerves wouldn't let her. She'd study enough to not make a fool of herself at this competition, or she'd die trying.

"Hello?" she said absently, without looking at who was calling.

"Miss? The car is here for you."

"The car?"

"To pick you up, miss. For dinner with Mr. Cambridge."

"Oh, jeez. I'm so sorry, Harold. I'll be right there."

"Yes, miss."

Victoria ended the call and jumped up from the Henry VII vintage writing desk tucked in her sitting room, which she mostly used as a study area. She hurried to change into a midnight blue cashmere sweater and cream-colored silk scarf, dark jeans, and chestnut leather Chanel boots before hurrying to the parking lot, the documents she needed him to sign tucked into her Birkin bag. Climbing into the car, Victoria slid across the dark leather seats and settled in to the heated car. Her father was meeting her at the restaurant—he had a late meeting in Los Angeles and would be heading to dinner with her directly from the office. Victoria toyed with the handles of her purse and leaned back against the seat. She'd been so busy practicing for the competition that she'd given little thought to the mechanisms of asking her father—or maybe it was just that she hadn't wanted to think about asking him. On top of everything else she was worried about, her dad's reaction was an additional concern she just couldn't deal with. Hopefully, tonight would go well, and he wouldn't mind that Victoria was spending her time and energy on something so far outside the realm of the family business. Everything Richard Cambridge did, and everything he'd ever expected of Victoria, was related to that business. His reaction to her spending time, even on something so trivial as an extracurricular type of activity, was hard for Victoria to predict.

"We've arrived, miss."

Victoria looked up to see they were parked outside of Verve, a new restaurant and club her father held a significant investment in. There was a line around the block to get inside, and the sleek black doors were open to the throng of people, flanked by bouncers and guards. Victoria exited the car and was led directly inside, and for the first time she looked at the line of people who were waiting to enter before she was ushered through the doors. There were a few girls waiting near the front with bored looks on their faces as they scrolled through their phones, and behind them was what looked like a family, and a couple laughing together. She only caught a glimpse, a blur of faces in the line, before Victoria and her dad's bodyguards entered the foyer. It was strange to think that she'd never given much thought before to the people who stood in line as she walked right in to a restaurant, or a club, or anywhere, essentially, that she wanted to go. It was normal to her, but it wasn't exactly fair, was it?

Richard was waiting at the bar, a martini glass in front of him. He stood immediately when he saw Victoria, and the bodyguards nodded as he approached.

"Mr. Cambridge, sir."

"You're late," he said tersely, eyeing the guards. "Why are you late?"

Knowing her father's propensity for firing people for the most minor of transgressions, Victoria stepped in.

"I was still dressing when they got there, Dad. It took me a while to get to the car."

"You're sure? They didn't arrive late?"

"I'm sure. I was just slow."

Richard's shoulders relaxed, and he nodded.

"Alright then."

Still, he gave the two bodyguards a stern glance as he led Victoria to a private table on the second floor.

"The restaurant looks popular, Dad," said Victoria, as the waiter poured water into their goblets. "I like the vibe. It's very modern."

"I'm glad you like it," said Richard, snapping his fingers at another waiter. "I think the décor is suitable. And the popularity can only mean good things for the investors."

"I just meant it was a cool place, Dad, but sure," said Victoria, and Richard chuckled. He scanned the menu briefly, and as Victoria did the same, she could already predict what he'd order. When another uniformed waitress walked past them, he snapped his fingers again and started to order. The girl's eyes widened as she seemed to figure out who he was, and to her credit, she grabbed her pad and started scribbling furiously as Richard ordered.

"We'll take two orders of the oysters on the half shell, with lemon. Then we'll have an order of the fig and olive tapenade, the prosciutto-wrapped asparagus, and the charcuterie board. For entrées she'll have the lobster tails and buttered spring salad, and I'll have the garlic herb prime rib. Keep the diet sodas coming for my daughter, here, and I'll take an ice water."

Victoria sighed, and relinquished her menu, eyeing the cold Moroccan-spiced salmon she would've preferred to try. Her dad had been doing this at restaurants for years—sometimes she was able to sneak an order in, but most of the time he chose what he thought would be best. It was useless to argue.

"So, how are things going, Dad?" said Victoria, as the waitress brought her a diet soda.

"Oh just fine, honey, just fine."

"Busy?"

"Always."

It was true. In all her years with him, Victoria had never seen her father sleep more than four hours a night. He was like a robot with a little-known weakness for chocolate chip cookies.

"And how's Maureen?"

"Oh, she's great," said Richard, smiling warmly, and Victoria blinked at the sincerity she heard in his voice.

"Really?"

"Yeah. She's at the London townhouse right now. I'm going to meet her there in a few days. I'll be there for a while on business. I wanted to see you before I left, since I'll be out of the country. I'll be finalizing a lot of the details for that new movie I told you about last time we met, actually, so I'll make sure to update you as needed."

Victoria nodded, sipping on her drink. She missed her dad when he left, she always did, but she was so used to it that it was second nature. Sometimes months would go by while he was away. But he always came back. It was a little surprising to hear him so happy with Maureen, though. Victoria was glad; she really did like her. Maybe Maureen would end up sticking around. Victoria ignored the part about the movie. It was just too overwhelming to delve into that. It would be better to deal with things one at a time. Plus, she probably wouldn't need to read for a part for months to come, so she had time to get everything else worked out in the meantime.

"So, how's school, Victoria?"

Their appetizer trays had just arrived; as the waiters set the oysters on their bed of ice down on the table, followed by the next several plates, Victoria choked on an ice cube in her drink.

"Well, uh," she started, "I actually wanted to talk to you about that, Dad."

"Oh, really? About what exactly?"

Richard chose an oyster; absently, Victoria mimicked his action.

"There are just a few forms I need you to sign, for something next week. I'm going to Riverside for the day on a sort of field trip."

"So, you need me to sign the typical off-campus pass, is that it?"

"Yeah, sort of. Well, that, and then a couple other forms that let me participate in this mandatory school thing that we're doing there."

Victoria knew she was being vague, and she was practically stammering, but she hadn't realized that she'd be this nervous to be honest. It just seemed impossible that this would be something her father understood, but she had to try.

"Do you need me to get you out of it? I don't

need you wasting your time on something pointless, especially since it's your senior year. I can write you an excuse slip if you want it, honey."

"No, you don't have to do that, Dad. I actually do want to go. It's this competition for math."

"A math competition? They have you kids doing the weirdest things now."

"I guess, but like I said, I do want to go."

"I just don't understand all these general education requirements," Victoria's dad continued, as if he hadn't heard her. "There's no need to push a student like you into something that'll have no applicability to their life after high school. It's just ridiculous."

"Dad, it's fine. You're not listening to me. I'm trying to tell you that—"

"You just let me know if you need any help getting out of any silly requirements, honey." Richard glanced at his cell phone, which had just lit up. "Here, let me sign those before I take this."

He scribbled his signature on her forms without

even glancing at the text, and then stood up from the table to take the call. Victoria heard him tersely begin to ask if the project was finished yet as he headed to the balcony, and she sagged in her chair. Well, that hadn't gone very well. He wouldn't even listen to her. Victoria glanced down at her signed forms. Maybe she should just be glad that he'd signed them and not worry about the logistics. Really, did it matter whether or not he knew she was competing with a school team? He definitely didn't make it sound like it was important to him. Just as she'd suspected, he thought it was a waste of her time.

Well, this whole Math Mania thing is temporary, thought Victoria, sipping on her soda. *I guess there's really no reason to bore him with the details now that he's signed the forms. What he doesn't know can't hurt him, right?*

You'll have to talk to him about this eventually, said that annoying little voice in Victoria's head. *Sometime, you'll have to tell him the path he sees you on and the path you want for yourself aren't the same anymore.*

"Sorry about that, honey," said Richard as he returned to the table. "Where were we?"

"Well, Dad—"

"Why aren't the entrées here yet?" Richard barked at another server, and Victoria sighed. It was probably just best to drop the subject for now. She toyed with the straw in her drink, and waited for her lobster tails to arrive.

Chapter Eight

For the first time in her life that she could remember, Victoria was awake before her alarm went off on Friday morning. She'd been lying in her bed, awake, for what seemed like hours before the alarm went off on her iPhone. Rolling over in bed, she turned off the alarm and sat up. It was the day of the Math Mania competition, and she was terrified.

Victoria got up and took a shower, just like any other morning. In fact, she kept trying to convince herself that today was like any other day, but her hands still shook as she brushed her hair. It took her ten minutes to find her shoes because she was so distracted.

What if she got up there and made a total fool of herself?

What if she couldn't answer any of the questions?

What if she answered one incorrectly and lost the match for the entire team?

As she tugged on her uniform, Victoria tried taking deep breaths. The charter bus would be here soon to take her and the rest of the Math Mania team to Riverside. She'd turned in all her permission slips to Mrs. Gable, and she was excused from all her classes. All her friends thought that she was out shopping with her stepmother. It wasn't her best excuse, but she'd been too distracted to come up with anything better.

Victoria grabbed her books in case she wanted to do any last-minute preparations on the bus. Tucking her cell phone into the front pocket of her backpack, Victoria locked the door of her suite behind her and started determinedly down the hall, refusing to acknowledge her shaking legs.

It's going to be fine, she told herself. *Just chill out. This is no big deal; it's just a dumb competition. I'm not even a real teammate.*

The rest of the girls had been really nice to her, though. Not that she cared, really. But she'd been to every practice in the past week or so, preparing for the competition, and they weren't so bad. Mostly she knew them from tutoring, or just being around Mrs. Gable so much, but they were good teammates. The girls were all pretty shy, and had been essentially terrified of Victoria when she first showed up. She couldn't blame them for that—Victoria Cambridge joining the Math Mania team would leave a lot of people shell-shocked, not least of all these poor little introverts too afraid to say "boo" to a goose, let alone to her. But as they'd gotten used to her being there, and accepted the fact that she wasn't going to tease them about their—in Victoria's opinion—largely questionable hairstyles or total lack of makeup, they'd warmed up to her. A couple of them actually had funny senses of humor, in a geeky way.

Victoria saw Mrs. Gable and her teammates waiting in the school's foyer for the charter bus and headed in their direction, with a covert look left and right first to make sure no one would see her leaving with the Math Mania team. Everyone was in the first class of the day, though, so the coast was clear.

"Good morning, Victoria," said Mrs. Gable. A couple girls smiled at her as she approached. Angelica, a second-year who had taken three practices to speak to Victoria at all, looked like she was ready to puke.

"Good morning," Victoria returned. Under her breath, she said, "Is Angelica okay?"

Mrs. Gable smiled wryly. "She's just a little nervous. Competition days are hard on her."

"I feel a little anxious myself," Victoria admitted.

"You're going to do great. There's nothing to

worry about. Just go up there and do the best you can. That's all you can do, anyway."

Victoria nodded; as she surveyed the small team, she could see that most of the girls looked just as nervous as she was, and they'd all done this before. It somehow made her feel a little better that she wasn't alone in her nerves. Everyone was in the same boat as she was, and they were all much shyer than Victoria. Victoria wasn't afraid of the stage, or of the crowd. She was more worried about answering a question wrong, or looking stupider than everyone else. These girls had straight up stage fright, and that was harder to fight. At least that wasn't a fear Victoria shared.

"The bus is here, girls," said Mrs. Gable. "Here we go. Danielle, don't forget your backpack."

Victoria chose a seat near the back. Originally she'd been irritated that she wouldn't be allowed to take a car of her own to the competition, but now, it was sort of nice that they were all traveling together. It made her feel like she wasn't alone. She was part of a team. Pulling her wireless headphones over her ears, Victoria settled in for the drive with her Calculus book on her lap. A tap on her shoulder had her taking her headphones off, frowning. It was Angelica.

"Do you mind if I sit next to you and study? I left my book in my room and I really don't want to just sit here in agony the whole drive."

Her face was earnest and drawn, and Victoria felt a stab of pity.

"Sure. I don't mind."

Angelica slid into the seat next to Victoria, flipping to the section on derivatives. Victoria glanced over occasionally, but mostly she listened to her music and just tried to focus on calming herself down. Everyone was so nervous. Someone had to be confident enough to set an example, and the best bet was Victoria. She might be the newest girl on the team, but she was also the bravest in front of a crowd. So, she needed to step up. Victoria watched the buildings flash by as they drove, and she hoped she wouldn't let the team down.

It took a few hours with traffic to reach the host high school in Riverside that they were competing against. Riverside Prep, also an all-girls school, wasn't as luxurious as Beverly Hills, Victoria decided as she critically eyed the exterior, but it was much larger. The auditorium was huge, with a domed ceiling and a polished wooden stage set up with stations for the judge and for each team.

"How many teams were originally competing for this slot?" Victoria asked.

"About ten," answered Mrs. Gable. "Now it's down to just the two of us, and whoever wins this round will go to state finals. It's the first year we've made it all the way to the semifinals," she finished, pride in her voice. "Sure, we won't win today, but that's fine. Making it here at all is historic for our school, and certainly something to be proud of."

"What if we do win?"

Mrs. Gable smiled.

"Then, we'd go to state in about six weeks. But, I don't want you getting your hopes up, Victoria. It's much more likely that this will be the end of the road for us this season. The Riverside team is very competent, and they've made it to the state finals for two of the past three years."

Victoria nodded, straightening her uniform slightly. She was proud to see that compared to the Riverside uniforms she saw on the opposing team, the one for Beverly Hills Prep was by far the sharpest. Victoria didn't think that would comfort anyone on her team, but it made her feel a little bit better. So what if it was a little shallow?

After Mrs. Gable guided the team through check-in, they headed to their section of the auditorium rows. Mrs. Gable would watch from here with the alternates as the five girls competed from the stage.

"We'll begin in about twenty minutes," said Mrs. Gable. "Now, I want everyone to take a deep breath, and make sure to use the restroom now if you need to go. I don't want anyone leaving this area for any reason once we're ten minutes away from start time."

Victoria glanced around at her teammates. Angelica's face was ashy, and Danielle's lips moved as she sat and recited theorems in her seat. Victoria looked up at the stage, and surveyed the parents and other official-looking people she assumed were school faculty in the crowd. All in all, this really wasn't so bad. She'd been in the spotlight her entire life. As long as she remembered even a fraction of what she'd been studying for the past few weeks, she would be fine. Now that the moment had arrived, Victoria felt much calmer.

A bell dinged, and everyone's eyes turned to the stage.

"Contestants, please take your places onstage," said a voice over the loudspeaker. "The competition will commence in five minutes."

"Okay, this is it," said Mrs. Gable. "Good luck, everyone. Head up to the stage now."

Victoria led the group through the aisle and to the steps leading to the stage. As she ascended, her sense of calm increased. There weren't a lot of people in the crowd, and the other team looked nervous, too. She moved to her position at the end of the long table. Each station was equipped with sharpened pencils, plenty of graph and regular paper, and an advanced graphing calculator. There was a microphone in front of each station for contestants to answer the questions. Victoria stood in her place and watched the judge walk to his place in the center. The questions would be projected onto the screen lowered in the center of the stage.

"Are the contestants ready?" All the girls nodded. Victoria picked up a pencil and made sure her calculator was ready. The judge dinged the starting bell, and an equation appeared on the projector board. It was complicated, but familiar to Victoria—she'd just gone over this particular theorem the day before. Writing furiously, she typed on her calculator and tried to solve it. Just as she was about to finish, the other team answered.

"That is correct," said the judge, and Victoria cursed inwardly. She'd been so close. There was a fifteen-second interval, and then the next question was projected—a derivative proof. Victoria worked even faster, letting her instincts take over, and when she solved it, she leaned into the microphone. To her shock, her own voice rang out first, and the judge nodded that her answer was correct.

"Team Beverly Hills Prep, that answer is correct. We are on to the last question of this round."

Victoria was exhilarated. She loved how fast the questions went, because there was so little time to stress about each one. By the time she'd worked through it, it was on to the next one, and her brain flew to keep up. Angelica answered a question, and

Danielle piped in, and Victoria answered another two on her own. The other team was very fast, too, and they chimed in rapidly, keeping the score neck and neck as the rounds progressed.

Victoria's hands were smudged from her pencil and she drank from the glass of ice water on the table as she waited for the next question. They were nearing the final rounds, and the blur of questions were becoming more and more complex. Victoria answered one correctly about matrices, and the other team fired back with a correct answer on limits. As they continued, each team struggled to stay focused as they became fatigued and the problems increased in complexity.

Finally, the last round arrived. Victoria's mind was buzzing, and she drank more water, trying to clear her head. If she could just focus on the next three questions, the competition would be over, and whatever the outcome, she'd be done.

Last round, she told herself. *This is the last one, and then you're finished.*

"This is the final round," the judge announced. "The score as it stands is fourteen points, Beverly Hills Prep, and thirteen points, Riverside. Let's begin the last round."

Victoria barely heard the score; she was too busy copying down the equation that had come onto the screen and solving it as quickly as she could. Letting her brain take over, she worked steadily, step-by-step, until she came to the end, certain that someone else would beat her to the punch. As her pencil scrawled her final answer, she leaned to shout it into her microphone, but a girl from the other tem beat her by a half-second. Victoria listened to her heart beating in her ears as they all waited for the judge to deliberate.

"That is correct," he announced, and she bit her lip anxiously. She'd been too slow. One of her teammates came back and answered the next question, a proof complicated enough to make Victoria's head spin, and then they were behind by one point again. The final question came up on the board, and the problem asked to find the domain of convergence for the designated series. Victoria closed her eyes as she searched her mind for that particular equation, and began to type into her calculator as it came to her.

The auditorium was completely silent except for the sound of pencils scratching on paper and the furious clicking as girls typed on their calculators. The minutes stretched on as the girls worked their way through the final problem, and as Victoria came to the conclusion of hers, she hesitated. This was a difficult problem, and she wasn't sure she was correct. If she had time to go back and check her work . . .

A girl on the other team leaned forward, and Victoria acted without thinking. She blurted her answer into her own microphone just a split-second before the other girl, but their answers were different. Victoria's palms began to sweat as the judge considered her answer; *what if the other girl was right?* She would've lost the competition for her entire team. The judge looked over at Victoria, and her stomach plummeted.

"Beverly Hills Prep, your answer is correct. The final score of the match is Beverly Hills Prep, sixteen points, Riverside, fourteen points. Therefore, I announce Beverly Hills Prep as the winner of the match!"

Victoria wanted to throw up and cry at the same time. The crowd burst into applause, and Victoria lined up to shake hands with the girls on the other team. Then Angelica hugged her, and then Danielle, and she saw Mrs. Gable was cheering from her seat in the crowd. They'd won.

Oh, no, thought Victoria. *We won. We actually won.*

Chapter Nine

The bus ride back to Beverly Hills Prep was euphoric. Victoria had never seen the other girls chatter so much, or so loudly, and Mrs. Gable couldn't stop smiling. Victoria was overwhelmed with the relief she felt knowing the match was over. It was so wonderfully satisfying to know she'd had some part, however small, in the team's success. Sara, the girl who'd been out because of her appendix, would be recovered in time for state finals, so Victoria assumed that this was where her association with the team ended.

Thank goodness, Victoria thought. *Now I don't*

have to stress myself out over math anymore. What a relief.

But it was a mixed relief. The stress was gone, replaced by happiness that they'd done so well, but a part of Victoria was disappointed that her time with the team was over. It was hard to admit, but it was true. It wasn't as though she'd even wanted to be part of the team in the first place, but now that she'd experienced it, it would be hard to give up.

I just didn't know that I'd love competing so much, Victoria thought. The match had gone by so fast, but it had been more exhilarating than she would've believed possible. *I mean, it was just math problems, but it was still exciting.* She'd been too focused to even be nervous once the competition had begun, and she hadn't done half-bad. The number of questions she answered surprised even her. Sure, she'd studied nonstop for what felt like forever, but she was pleasantly surprised at how much information she'd retained.

They arrived back at the school, and Mrs. Gable went to the front of the bus as they parked.

"Ladies, you did an excellent job today. I'm very proud of each and every one of you. The state finals are in six weeks, and we're going to work even harder until that day comes. I want everyone to make sure to schedule more time in the afternoons for longer practices and more on the weekends, as well. You were amazing up there today. For this weekend, just relax, and we'll start preparing harder than ever next week."

The girls cheered, and the chatter continued as they all filed off the bus. Victoria grabbed her stuff and joined the line. As she reached the front of the bus, Mrs. Gable turned to her and smiled.

"Victoria, please come by my office tonight after dinner."

"Tonight?"

"I know it'll be late, and you're tired, so I apologize in advance for that. But yes, tonight, if you have the time."

Victoria nodded. "I have time. I'll see you then."

Why would Mrs. Gable want to talk to me? Victoria wondered. Her work with the team was done, and they'd done well today. It wasn't like she'd want to yell at her for messing things up for the team or something like that.

Victoria glanced around as they departed the bus, but all the other students were either at dinner or on the grounds somewhere, and she didn't think anyone saw her leaving with the Math Mania team. She hadn't explicitly asked the other girls on the team not to talk about the fact that she'd been at the competition with them, because it felt too lame, and she didn't want them to think she cared if people knew. But none of them had a ton of friends to tell, anyway, so she doubted it would be an issue.

After dropping off her bag and the rest of her stuff in her suite, Victoria headed straight to the dining hall. On Friday nights they periodically served themed cuisine, and today it was an all-sushi menu. Victoria loaded her silver tray with yellowtail sashimi, a spicy tuna roll with cucumber, another specialty roll covered in seared salmon and white tuna, and plenty of ginger and wasabi. Choosing a pair of hand-carved chopsticks and a linen napkin, she ambled over to the table where her friends were sitting and grabbed the organic soy sauce in its ceramic bottle.

"How was shopping today, Victoria?" asked Annabelle. "Did you find anything on Rodeo Drive?"

"Oh, of course. I picked up tons of stuff," said Victoria, mixing wasabi into her soy sauce bowl. "I think I got seven new pairs of shoes."

"Anything in black? I need a new pair for a function my parents are making me go to this weekend."

"Nothing new in black, but you can look through my old shoes if you want."

"Seven new pairs, and none in black?"

"Yup," said Victoria brightly, but she saw Annabelle's eyes narrow slightly. It was beginning to become lost on her why she'd ever become friends with her in the first place. Had Annabelle always been this, well, unpleasant? *I guess I just never really cared before*, Victoria thought. It seemed like everything was changing. She felt different, somehow. Annabelle had probably always acted like this, but Victoria either hadn't noticed or hadn't cared, but now . . . now Annabelle was the same, but Victoria was different. The things she cared about had changed when she wasn't paying attention. It was an unsettling feeling.

Victoria absentmindedly finished her sushi and her diet soda with a straw, and left the dining hall. The day was catching up with her, and Victoria was dreaming of going to sleep early and sleeping in until noon the next day. As she unlocked her suite, she remembered that she was supposed to see Mrs. Gable, and sighed. She thought she'd done well today, but maybe the teacher had some criticism for her about the match. Victoria changed into her designer sweats with the Beverly Hills Prep logo and tied her hair up in a high ponytail. Then, she left her room for what she hoped was the last time that night to go and see what Mrs. Gable needed to talk to her about.

Chapter Ten

"Come in, Victoria," said Mrs. Gable as Victoria knocked, and she let herself into the teacher's classroom.

"Hi, Mrs. Gable," said Victoria, sitting down in the chair on the other side of the polished deck. "You wanted to see me?"

"Yes, yes, I did. First of all Victoria, I wanted to congratulate you for today."

"Thanks," said Victoria. "It wasn't just me, though. It was all of us."

"It was a team effort, certainly, but I was particularly impressed by you."

Something about Mrs. Gable's direct gaze was making Victoria squirm.

"You are the newest official member of the team, by far, and you had a very limited amount of time to practice. All of that aside, you answered the most questions correctly today of anyone else on the team, and you didn't answer any incorrectly. Not a single one."

"Okay," said Victoria. "I mean, yeah, all that is true, I guess. I wasn't keeping track of how many questions I answered. Should I have let the other girls answer more?"

"No, not at all. I thought you showed real leadership today, and on top of that, you showed enormous skill. I was very, very impressed, and so were several of the admissions officers in attendance."

"There were admissions officers there?"

"Oh, yes. Several from Caltech, and others from across the country."

"I hadn't even thought of that," said Victoria.

"I remember you saying they could be there, but I guess I was just so nervous that it slipped my mind."

"I spoke with a couple of them after you competed. You impressed them, too. They knew of you because of your family, but had no idea that this was an avenue you were pursuing. The word from those who know your father is that you'll go into the family business, as such, when you graduate."

"Yeah, well, I can see why people would expect that," said Victoria. "It's not like I've been making waves on the Math Mania team for years like some of the other girls. This was my first competition."

"I understand that, and I let the admissions officers know. They were cautious to place faith in someone so newly interested in the STEM fields, but I assured them that you were one of my best students and that you'd been involved in the math department here, unofficially, for years."

"Wow," said Victoria. "Thank you. I mean—you didn't have to do that."

"It was my pleasure, Victoria."

"I just don't have a lot of other people to talk to about this, like, part of my life," Victoria admitted. "So, it's strange to have other people discussing it besides me and you, I guess."

"Your father isn't involved in your interests?"

"No, he is, but this is something that I haven't really considered legitimate," said Victoria. "That sounds bad—I just thought of it more as a hobby, I guess. And I don't know that he'd understand if I tried to talk to him about actually pursuing something like this."

"Well, Victoria, you should consider how you want to approach that," said Mrs. Gable gently. "This could be a very viable avenue for you. I think you could do very well at a school where you'd learn to hone your skills."

Victoria chewed on her lip. It was a lot to think about.

"You asked me once if I thought that you could do this," the teacher continued. "And I said I did. And today, you proved me right. You have what it takes to excel in whatever career you could want in math, or physics. I know you enjoy physics a lot—maybe an engineering career is in your future. But for now, I'd like to focus on your present. And I'd like to invite you to compete with the Math Mania team again at the state finals."

Victoria just blinked. She brought a hand up to cover her mouth as she started smiling.

"Oh, my gosh. Really?"

"Yes, really. You more than earned a spot, today. I think it's only fair that the person who worked as hard as you did to help in the semifinals is there to help us win the state finals."

"You don't really think we could win state, do you?" said Victoria. "I mean, you didn't even think we had a chance at semifinals."

"I didn't think we'd win because I'd never seen you compete," said Mrs. Gable, and Victoria's heart swelled with pride. "But with you, I think it's possible. I've spoken to Sara—she's still recovering from surgery, and she doesn't mind. So, start preparing for another competition."

"Okay," said Victoria excitedly. "I'll do my best."

"Last time I asked you to do this, you refused, before you changed your mind," said Mrs. Gable, smiling. "This time, you actually seem excited."

"Well, I had a lot of fun today," admitted Victoria. "I was surprised how much I liked it."

"You're also very good at it," said Mrs. Gable, "so I'm glad to hear that. It's been great having you as part of this team, Victoria, and I mean that. You've worked hard, and it shows."

"Thank you," said Victoria. "Wow. That means a lot. Today has been so crazy, but I'm so glad that it worked out like it did. I can't believe we have another competition to prepare for now."

Mrs. Gable nodded, launching into her plans for the team's practices and strategies leading up to state finals.

Victoria took a deep breath; she was feeling very tired, and overwhelmed, and Mrs. Gable's words were making her head spin. Not only had she competed in her first competition today, but she'd excelled. *What could that mean for me?* Funny, this time around she hadn't even considered turning Mrs. Gable down. Now that she'd had a taste of what competing was like, she was glad Mrs. Gable had asked her back for state finals.

I could help them win, Victoria thought. *I mean, I could help us win. Today was so amazing, and it was nothing like I expected it to be.*

Maybe what Mrs. Gable was saying was true, about how she could have a future in a field like this. There were admissions officers there today, after all.

Victoria leaned back in her seat and sighed. There was just so much to think about. But at the very least, she hadn't embarrassed herself today. Instead, the team was headed to the state finals, with Victoria along for the ride. She just wished she knew if that was a good thing or not.

Chapter Eleven

Spring always seemed to come early at Beverly Hills Prep; just a few weeks after the semifinals, it was warm enough for Victoria to loop her sweater around her waist and still feel toasty in her crisp button-up uniform as she walked across the grounds to lunch. The beginning of the year had held mostly gloomy, drizzly days with gray skies, but now that spring was arriving, clouds were replaced with sunshine, and Victoria was not at all sad to see the rain go. Sure, living in Southern California meant that she enjoyed many more days of sunshine than much of the rest of the world, but that was the way she liked it. One drizzly day was enough to make her feel depressed—this warm spring weather was a much better alternative.

Victoria practically bounced into the dining hall, snagging a silver tray and perusing her menu options for that afternoon. Thankfully, the Valentine's Day themes had finally been taken down, and they weren't serving only red and pink food items anymore. It seemed like she'd eaten cherry cream-filled tarts and fluffy strawberry shortcake for days on end before they quit on the color scheme. Today, there were broccoli tartlets and deviled egg appetizers with parsley, a vegan and vegetarian soup and wrap combo, and a variation of gourmet sandwiches for the main entrée. Victoria chose tuna salad on an artisanal sourdough roll crusted in rosemary and sea salt, sliced apple pieces with a side of melted caramel, and of course a diet soda with one of the leftover pink straws from Valentine's Day.

As she walked with her tray over to her usual

table, Victoria noticed some odd glances coming her way. A few girls at a neighboring table leaned their heads together, whispering, and as Victoria glanced over at them they looked away quickly, chattering to each other.

Do I have a sign on my back or something? Victoria thought. *Well, whatever. It's not like I'm not used to being stared at—or talked about for that matter. It's just that usually I know why people are doing it.*

As she set her tray down and settled into her seat next to Sasha and Lulu, Annabelle reached over the table and poked her arm, hard.

"Ow, Annabelle," said Victoria, rubbing at her elbow. "What was that for?"

"I just thought you should know that something very interesting came out today in the Beverly Hills Prep Daily," said Annabelle, her voice breathy with excitement.

"The school newspaper? That's wonderful, Annabelle," replied Victoria, taking a bite of her sandwich.

"I'm sure it's a typo of some kind," said Annabelle. "I mean, it has to be. There's just no way it can be true." She was practically shaking, and Victoria knew this kind of excitement over something was usually because it related to gossip. *What did she know?*

"What's a typo?" asked Vivi, leaning into the conversation.

"This article that came out in today's edition. Here, Victoria—why don't you take a look? I'm sure you're going to want to write in and correct the error. It would be way too embarrassing to just let people think this was true."

Victoria tugged the paper toward her. There was an article on the new health and wellness center, a photo of the lacrosse team winning a match, and an editorial on the baked goods offered by the chefs in the dining halls.

"Nothing in here looks that interesting to me," said Victoria. She flipped to the next page, and then the next, and then she saw it.

It was a small photo in black and white, thankfully hidden near the bottom of the page. Underneath it, there was a paragraph that detailed the match the Math Mania team had narrowly won against a rival team a couple of weeks prior, a match that landed them an opportunity to go to state finals for the first time in twenty years. The photo was taken from the audience, and it depicted the teams on either side of the stage, with the judge in the center. The photo looked as though it had been snapped mid-match, as there was a problem on the projector and someone in the back of the photo was leaning in to answer. Victoria squinted—you couldn't really tell that she was in the photo, since she was the furthest from the camera, but in the description, the team member's names and year were listed.

Victoria Cambridge, senior.

"Is that your name, Victoria?" asked Lulu. "I mean, I know it's listed there, but that's wrong, isn't it?"

Victoria's heart pounded. She looked up at Annabelle, who was practically salivating with curiosity, and then to Lulu, who just looked confused. Vivi rested her chin in her hands, looking at Victoria expectantly, but with no judgment. And for a moment, Victoria wondered why she'd ever cared whether people knew she was on the Math Mania team. She'd never had any issue with making waves in her life before—why would she be nervous to reveal this truth about herself?

Maybe because it's just so far from anything I've ever tried before, Victoria thought. *When you tell people you've acted in movies, it's a different response than when you tell people you love math. It's so, well, geeky. But I don't care. I've never cared what other people thought of me—and this can't be any different.*

"No, that isn't a typo," said Victoria. "That's a photo of the Math Mania team, and I'm right there in the back. And they listed my name as a team member because I'm on the team."

Not just Victoria's table went quiet; it seemed as

though the entire dining hall had gone still as other girls overheard Victoria's words. For a moment that felt like an eternity, it was quiet, and then normal chatter resumed. Victoria arched her eyebrows expectantly at Annabelle, who had gone pale.

"That's really cool, Victoria," said Vivi. "I knew you were good enough to help us with our homework, but I didn't know you were such a math whiz. That's awesome."

Annabelle spluttered slightly, and Lulu smirked at her.

"Thanks," said Victoria, slightly relieved. "I haven't been a member for long—I basically just did it because Mrs. Gable asked me to."

"I can't believe you didn't say anything about it," Annabelle finally said. Victoria shrugged.

"I guess I thought you might think it was embarrassing or something," she said, and Annabelle had the grace to blush. "But there's no hiding it now, and I don't want to act like I'm ashamed of it when I'm not."

"That's cool," said Lulu, and everyone else nodded, affirming her words.

"Yeah, Victoria. We don't care that you're on an academic team. It's just like you said—most of us are on either gymnastics or dance. It's really no different," Vivi said.

"Yeah, and you can actually help me with my homework when I get stuck on a math problem that no one else can figure out," said Lulu.

Everyone laughed, and the tension dissipated. Victoria sipped on her soda, noting that Annabelle still looked a little scandalized, but that was to be expected. She was the most judgmental out of the entire group, and Victoria was a little disappointed in herself that she once considered her a close friend. Annabelle could be loyal, but she wasn't always supportive, and that made being her friend hard. Plus, Victoria always had the feeling that Annabelle liked her more because of who her dad was than who she really was on her own, regardless of her family's name.

Victoria took another bite of her sandwich as the conversation went back to normal topics. That hadn't been as difficult as she'd expected at all. Actually, the worry that everyone would find out had been worse than everyone finding out.

Maybe it's a sign, thought Victoria. *Maybe it means that I'm supposed to be doing this, that I'm on the right track. Should I try talking to my dad about it again?*

Her dad had been out of the country for a couple of weeks now, and Victoria didn't think he would be back for a while still. So, for now, it seemed to work best for him not to know. It wasn't as though the time she'd tried to talk to him about it had gone well, anyway. Since the dinner, Victoria had spoken to her dad on the phone or on FaceTime several times, but she hadn't tried bringing the subject up again. It was strange—Victoria hadn't realized how much their relationship had revolved around discussing the family business until she'd stepped outside of it.

It'll be fine, Victoria told herself. *He'll understand.*

But what if he just wouldn't listen?

Victoria squashed the thought she was too afraid to answer.

Chapter Twelve

After her classes finished for the day, Victoria had a brief lull before she was due at Mrs. Gable's office for Math Mania practice. Scrolling idly through her phone, Victoria made a quick stop at the administrative office to pick up her mail on the way back to her suite. Each of the resident students had a little mailbox, gold-embossed with their first and last names in calligraphy. Victoria occasionally stopped by the administrative office in the evenings on her way to Study Hall, since it was on her route back to her room—and also because of the basket of chocolates that was always stuffed to the brim and readily available on the welcoming table. Well, the mail room was in there too, so no one could call her a glutton.

"Good evening, Ms. Cambridge," said the headmistress, emerging from her study as Victoria entered the main lobby.

"Oh, good evening, Headmistress Chambers," Victoria replied politely, grabbing a chocolate.

"I saw the editorial on the Math Mania team in the Daily," said the headmistress, pausing at the main doors. "Congratulations on the semifinals victory."

"Thank you, Headmistress," said Victoria. "Uh, it was my first competition, but I'm excited about the state finals."

"Yes, that is exciting news. Well, best of luck to you and the rest of the girls," she said, and then she was gone, walking regally down the hallway, greeting other students as she went.

Victoria absently unlocked her mailbox with her tiny key and retrieved the mail inside, stuffing it into her bag as she left the main lobby. Checking her watch as she neared the front door of her suite, Victoria calculated that she had enough time to change into casual dress for tonight's practice. She dropped her bag and keys on the glass side table and quickly changed into something more comfortable for practice. Ambling back over to her bag, Victoria opened it and took out her mail, idly flipping through the magazines and dropping them on her side table.

As she flipped through them, mentally reciting some theorems she'd been studying in preparation for Math Mania practice, Victoria looked down and realized she was holding a couple of envelopes. One was addressed from the Massachusetts Institute of Technology, and as she read the return address, her hands shook. This was her acceptance letter, or denial, from MIT.

Victoria plopped down onto her sitting room couch, clutching the envelope. It was strange to think how much her mindset had changed since she'd originally applied. When she'd filled out the applications, it had been a last-minute scramble to just get them done and sent in before she missed the deadline. There hadn't been time to worry, and Victoria had believed it was a last resort. But now, everything was different. Now, she could see herself with a life and a career in some of the fields a school like MIT could offer. That made the contents of this envelope that much more significant.

Hands shaking slightly, Victoria tore the envelope open as carefully as she could, inch by inch. When it was open, she hesitated again before reaching inside to pull out the letter. Taking a deep breath, Victoria held the letter to her chest for a moment. Then, she slowly unfolded it, her eyes jumping immediately to the first few lines.

Dear Ms. Cambridge,

The Massachusetts Institute of Technology thanks you for your application as an undergraduate student. Unfortunately, we regret to inform you that we are unable to accept you as a new student at this time . . .

Victoria read the sentence over and over again. Her heart felt as though it were stuck in her throat, and her eyes were hot and itchy. It was a denial letter, that much was abundantly clear, but she couldn't stop reading it, as though she could make the words change if she just stared at it hard enough. It wasn't that she was surprised to be denied, really—it was one of the top technical schools in the nation, and Victoria's grades weren't perfect. Her SAT scores were strong in math and science, but this was MIT.

I just can't believe I actually got my hopes up, she thought. *I should've known this wasn't a real possibility.*

Victoria stood up, pacing around the couch in an attempt to shake the terrible heaviness on her chest. Briefly, she considered calling her dad, but quickly dismissed the thought. He didn't even know she had applied, after all.

This doesn't mean anything, Victoria told herself. *This shouldn't upset you. It doesn't even matter.*

Pushing the thoughts from her mind, Victoria lifted her chin and gathered her books, locking the door behind her as she headed to Math Mania practice like nothing at all was wrong.

Victoria missed three sample questions in a row at Math Mania practice during the mock matchups. One-on-one with Danielle, she just couldn't focus on the problem in front of her as quickly as she usually could. She would get stalled in the middle of an equation that she had already memorized, or lose her train of thought and get stuck in the middle of a proof. After the third time that Danielle got to the answer before her, Mrs. Gable stopped the mock matchup.

"Great job, Danielle. That answer was correct. Why don't we have two others come to the front and try a few, please?"

Victoria blinked, and moved to the back of the classroom with Danielle and the rest of the team as the two new contestants got settled. Her mind was in a fog that she was having trouble clearing. If she could just stop thinking about the rejection letter for one minute, she would be able to focus on the math problems. Victoria took a deep breath, struggling to calm herself down. She bit her nails without realizing it, one after the other, and she didn't notice Mrs. Gable's concerned looks, either. The sentence rejecting her from MIT replayed in Victoria's head like a movie she couldn't turn off.

Finally, Mrs. Gable called an early end to the practice.

"Great work tonight, everyone," she said as the girls filed out. "I'll see you all tomorrow."

Victoria slung her bag over her shoulder and

turned to the door, but Mrs. Gable stopped her with a gentle hand on her arm.

"Victoria? Can you stay here for just a minute, please? I'll write you a pass so you won't get written up for being late to your room."

"Sure," Victoria muttered. She walked to the chair in front of Mrs. Gable's desk and plopped down, dropping her bag on the ground. Folding her arms, she waited for whatever Mrs. Gable had to say, her mind light years away.

"Victoria, is something wrong?"

"What do you mean?"

"You seem a little distracted."

Victoria shrugged. She was suddenly very afraid to speak at all; if she did, she wasn't sure she could keep her voice from breaking. Swallowing hard, Victoria struggled to reel in her emotions.

"I'm just tired," said Victoria. "I had a long day today. I'm sorry that I didn't do very well in the mock matchup."

"That's okay—I'm not worried about that right

now. I thought it seemed like something might be on your mind. I just wanted to let you know that I'm here to listen, if you feel like talking about it."

Victoria looked at Mrs. Gable, whose hair was pulled back into the usual severe knot. The teacher's hands were folded on her desk, and her eyes were kind. Victoria shook her head, her breath catching in her throat. She wasn't sure where to start. In her life, she didn't have many other girls to talk to about, well, anything, so this was a little hard.

"I got a letter from MIT today," said Victoria, knotting her hands together. "I didn't get in."

"Oh, Victoria, I'm sorry. It's always disappointing to get a rejection letter."

"It's not even a big deal," said Victoria, wiping her nose. "Like, I just applied on a whim. So, it shouldn't matter that I didn't get in."

"It's okay to feel upset," said Mrs. Gable. "That's completely understandable."

"I just feel so stupid," said Victoria, brushing away a tear. "I actually let myself get my hopes up that I could get in. Just because I'm okay at math doesn't mean I'm going to get into schools as good as MIT. I just feel like I waited too long to figure all this out. If I'd spent more time paying attention in school during my first couple years here, maybe I would've realized what I wanted to do earlier. I never even considered going to college anywhere but online until so recently. I just feel like I messed everything up."

"None of this is your fault," said Mrs. Gable. "The fact that you didn't get into MIT must be disappointing right now, but you can't hold this kind of regret against yourself. It's not going to make the situation any better to punish yourself for things you can't change."

"You don't think this is all just a big mistake I'm making?" asked Victoria. "I just feel like if this was supposed to work out, then I would've gotten into MIT."

"I don't think you can base your life choices on whether or not something should or shouldn't have happened based purely on fate," said Mrs. Gable slowly. "And no, by no means do I think you should take this as a sign to quit what you've been pursuing. There are other schools, Victoria."

"I probably won't get into any of them," said Victoria.

"Don't say that. You're a smart, capable person. This one rejection doesn't define you."

"I was surprised by how upset it made me," Victoria admitted. "I sort of hoped that it wouldn't affect me, you know? Like maybe that would mean that I didn't care about this as much as I actually do."

"Why would it be better if you cared less?"

"Because then I wouldn't be so upset. Because it wouldn't matter to me as much, I guess. It's hard to care about something and then be disappointed."

Victoria sighed, leaning back in her chair. She did feel better than she had when she first opened the rejection letter. Talking about it had helped.

"I guess there's one good thing about me getting

rejected. I don't have to try to explain to my dad that I got into MIT."

"Does he still not know about all this? What does he think you're going to do when you graduate?"

"Be in this new movie," said Victoria.

Mrs. Gable's eyes widened.

"Well, I still have to read for it, but that's the general plan—to go into the family business and work with him in that field, making movies and all that."

"Well, there are a lot of aspects in that business that require different types of math and engineering, aren't there?" said Mrs. Gable. "I imagine there are sound and lighting engineers, set engineers, production engineers, that all work on film sets."

"I guess I never seriously considered that option," said Victoria slowly. "I mean, I've dreamed about it, maybe. But we've always been so focused on having me in the spotlight that I never considered having me work in movies as anything other than an actress. I never thought it could actually happen; it just didn't seem plausible."

"And you don't want to be an actress anymore?"

"Not particularly," sighed Victoria, rubbing a hand over her face. "I just don't love being in front of the camera. I'm more interested in production and behind-the-scenes aspects, and editing. I've actually learned a lot about all of that just by being present on so many sets in my life."

"It sounds to me like you could still have a future in something both you and your father can enjoy," said Mrs. Gable. "It's definitely something for you to consider."

"Yeah," said Victoria slowly. Her head was spinning. "I've got a lot to think about."

Chapter Thirteen

"Hello. Earth to Victoria. Earth to Victoria."

"Huh?"

Victoria dropped the pencil she'd been holding as she jerked out of her daze. Vivi had been gently poking her from across the classroom aisle and she hadn't even noticed.

"It's your turn to read and translate," said Vivi, sliding her copy of *Hamlet* across the desk. "Are you ready?"

"Yeah, sorry," said Victoria, flipping to the correct page. "I'm ready."

A few minutes later, the bell rang, and Victoria

rose gratefully from her seat. It had been a week since her rejection letter from MIT arrived, and every day the state finals drew closer and closer. Victoria had been thinking about her options in the family industry ever since her meeting with Mrs. Gable. The idea that she could still work closely with her dad in the field they both loved was exhilarating, and nerve-wracking. She badly wanted to hear his advice and have his support on the topic, but she was still afraid to try being honest with him again. It was hard to think that he might not listen to her at all, the way he'd brushed her off at the restaurant.

Victoria knew he didn't mean to be gruff with her, but he was so busy all the time, and so focused on where he thought her future was headed, that sometimes it was like he didn't hear her at all. He was so convinced that they were on the same track, looking in the exact same direction, that Victoria wasn't sure what his reaction would be when she told him her new hopes for herself. All she could do was trust that he loved her, and hope that was enough to make him understand.

Anyway, Victoria thought, *I still have some time. State is coming up, but he doesn't need to know about that. And after that competition, the season is over, and then there's plenty of time before graduation to talk to him. It's going to be fine.*

Victoria walked across the grounds on her way back to her suite before yet another Math Mania practice. It had been taking up even more of her time as state finals neared and Mrs. Gable scheduled longer practices. But she felt much more prepared for the competition this time around. It had been weeks and weeks since she'd started practicing, and her confidence was much higher than it had been for the semifinals. The team was working more cohesively together and growing more comfortable with one another's skills and weaknesses, making them stronger as a unit.

Victoria walked around the large group of girls doing yoga in the botanical garden, their hands raised to the sky. Another few girls were lounging in the grass near the arboretum, tilting their faces to the sun. It was unseasonably warm, and Victoria wished she had more time to just sit out here awhile. It was disorienting to think that in another couple short months she'd be graduating from this place. Her first years here felt like they'd dragged on and on, and this one had flown by. It was probably because this year she'd focused on something she was really interested in, and when she'd first come here she thought she'd known everything already.

Victoria sighed, checking her watch. She wanted to go to the library for an hour or two before Math Mania practice. Most of the campus was architecturally historic, and it was all beautiful, but the library was exceptional. Victoria was going to miss the floor-to-ceiling windows and the silent, towering shelves even more than the amazing, melt-in-your-mouth truffles that the chefs made every week.

I never thought I'd miss the library most, Victoria thought. *A lot has changed since freshman year.*

As Victoria unlocked her suite and dropped her bag on the side table, a stack of papers slid out from underneath it and scattered across the floor.

"Great," Victoria muttered, leaning down to gather them up. They were mostly just notes and old homework, all stacked on her table. *I should've just thrown this all away weeks ago,* she thought, stuffing handfuls of paper into the miniature trash can near the door. As she lifted another handful of trash, a large envelope slipped from the middle of the pile and fell to the ground, sliding across the shining hardwood floor until it went under the couch. Bent down on her knees, Victoria reached for it irritably. It was addressed to her, she realized—why hadn't she seen this before? It must have gotten lost in the pile on the table.

Victoria's heart nearly stopped as she saw the return address. It was from Caltech.

When had this come? Victoria wondered, studying

the still-closed envelope. It must have arrived with the MIT letter, and she'd been so distracted she'd totally missed it. Victoria thought about the crushing disappointment of the MIT letter, and bit her lip. She was too afraid to open it. It was too much pressure, and last time had just been a major disappointment. Sure, she was curious, but she was also afraid of being rejected again. Victoria eyed the letter, lifting it up and down in an effort to check its weight. *It's definitely heavier than the MIT letter*, she decided. *But what does that mean? Is that good or bad?*

Victoria sighed, flipping the letter over and over in her hands. She wasn't in the mood to open it right now. Maybe later would be better, when she was feeling braver. For the time being, she stuffed it into the front pocket of her bag and zipped the pocket closed. It was time for Math Mania practice, anyway, so the letter would have to wait until later.

Victoria stopped quickly by the dining hall to request a specially-made, extra chocolatey-chocolate milkshake with strawberries in her own ceramic thermos before heading to practice. There was always a specialty chef on call for those sorts of requests, and Victoria wasn't ashamed to say she put in her fair share. She saw a few girls, including Lulu's roommate Marina, staring longingly at the milkshake as the chef poured it into her mug; sometimes Victoria thought she was the only girl in school not on some sort of low-fat diet.

The letter felt as though it was burning a hole in her bag as Victoria arrived at Mrs. Gable's classroom. It was just sitting there, waiting to be read. Victoria bit her lip, tugging her books and binders out in preparation for practice. As she pulled out her Calculus book, the letter fluttered gently to the floor. Sighing, Victoria reached for it at the same time as Danielle did.

"Here, Victoria, you dropped your letter," she said, and then she paused as she read the return address. "Wait. Is this from Caltech?"

"Yeah, it is," said Victoria, snatching the letter back. "I haven't opened it yet."

"I'm sorry, I didn't mean to butt into your business," said Danielle. "I just didn't know you applied. It's a great school. I'd love to go, someday."

"They probably rejected me, anyway," muttered Victoria.

"What if they didn't?" said Danielle. She smiled at Victoria as Mrs. Gable entered the room and announced that practice was starting.

As the rest of the team sat down at the surrounding desks and Mrs. Gable began to put sample problems up on the projector, Victoria took a moment to look around her. These girls had become her friends in the past few weeks, and Mrs. Gable had been more than a teacher. She'd introduced Victoria to a world she hadn't known existed, and Victoria was grateful for that.

As the bell on Mrs. Gable's desk dinged the end of the practice rounds, Victoria raised her hand as often as she could in an effort to beat her teammates to the answers. There was a playful rivalry between all of them now, and as often as Victoria was first to answer a question, someone else beat her to the next one. They'd come a long way since Victoria had just been helping the team out, that much was certain. Now she was a full-fledged team member, and it never ceased to amaze her how much she'd come to enjoy that.

I don't care what that letter says, thought Victoria. *Even if they do reject me, I'll still pursue this path. I still want to be an engineer. Whatever that letter says, they can't change that.*

The practice came to an end, and Mrs. Gable dismissed them after the final practice question. Girls began to file out of the classroom again, chatting with each other, and Victoria gathered her things to leave. As she began to put her books and calculator back into her bag, the letter seemed to stare at her from its place in an inside pocket. She reached for it, then hesitated and pulled her hand away, shaking her head.

"Is there something in that bag of yours with teeth, Victoria?" said Mrs. Gable. Victoria looked up, embarrassed, as the last girl filed out of the room.

"No," Victoria sighed, standing up from the desk. "Nothing with teeth. Just something I don't want to open."

"Can I ask what that might be?" the teacher said, shuffling through her lesson plans.

Victoria hesitated. "It's my letter from Caltech," she admitted, and the teacher's head snapped up.

"Your admission letter?"

"Or rejection letter," Victoria clarified. "I think I got it when I got the one for MIT, too, but this one got lost in my suite and I just found it today."

"Why don't you want to open it?"

"I just don't feel like opening another rejection letter tonight," said Victoria. "The last one was hard enough."

"You don't know this is a rejection letter, though," said Mrs. Gable.

"I know, but I'm afraid to hope that it's not," said Victoria. "I mean, I'm afraid either way. What if they accept me? That's a scary thought, too. Either way, my life will change."

"Change is hard," said Mrs. Gable. "But so is staying in the same place."

"I guess so," sighed Victoria.

"You don't have to open it tonight. Do what feels right to you. But at some point, you will need to know what that letter says."

Victoria reached into her bag again, ruffling through the loose paper and binders, and tugged the letter free.

"Will you open it for me?" she said. "I know it's weird, but I'm afraid to do it myself. And I don't have anyone else I can really trust with this kind of thing. I'm not ready for my friends to know that I applied to schools like this, but I did tell them that I'm on the Math Mania team."

"I'm glad to hear that," said Mrs. Gable, "but

I don't think I can open your letter for you. It's yours, not mine."

"Please, will you?" Victoria begged. "I'm too nervous. Just tell me what it says, and either way, it is what it is. It's okay. I just can't read it myself."

Mrs. Gable sighed, but she took the envelope that Victoria pushed at her.

"Are you sure about this?" she asked, and Victoria nodded.

"Yes, please. I'm scared to open it myself but I'm also too anxious to know what it says. I don't want to keep wondering."

"Okay, then," said Mrs. Gable, and she carefully slid the envelope open with her finger. Drawing the letter out, she glanced at Victoria, who was biting her nails anxiously, before reading the first line. There was a long silence—probably only a few seconds, but to Victoria it felt like an eternity.

"Well?" said Victoria, practically bouncing from foot to foot with nervous energy. "What does it say?"

She was afraid to know, but she was more afraid not to.

"You're sure you don't want to read it yourself?"

"Not yet. Please, just tell me, did they say yes or no?"

Victoria clenched her hands into fists to stop them from shaking.

"They said yes," said Mrs. Gable. "Victoria, they said yes."

Chapter Fourteen

Victoria's legs felt like they'd turned to jelly. There was a buzzing in her head, and her heart seemed to be beating ten times faster than normal. She gulped, fighting her dry throat, and croaked out, "Are you sure?"

"Yes, I'm sure," said Mrs. Gable, smiling broadly. She handed Victoria the letter back, and Victoria read it herself with shaking hands.

Dear Miss Victoria Cambridge,

The California Institute of Technology thanks you for your application, and we are pleased to inform you that you have been accepted into the undergraduate class of 2022. Details will be . . .

Victoria didn't read any further; her eyes were too fuzzy suddenly to be able to make out the words, anyway.

"I can't believe this," she whispered, and Mrs. Gable stood up from her desk to take Victoria's shoulders in her hands.

"Congratulations," said Mrs. Gable, and Victoria smiled up at her. "This is a huge moment."

"Thank you," said Victoria. "Thank you so much."

Then, she was spinning in circles in the middle of the classroom, laughing hysterically and practically leaping with joy with every step.

"I got in!" she screamed. "I got in! Oh, my gosh. I really can't believe it."

Mrs. Gable laughed, clasping her hands together.

"I'm very proud of you," she said. "I'm glad I

spoke to the Caltech representatives at the semifinals when I did!"

"Me too!"

Mrs. Gable nodded. "But it was important to temper expectations in case it didn't pan out. I didn't want to get your hopes up just to have you feel disappointed, and nothing was set in stone."

"What did you say to them?"

"They asked about your grades, specifically in your math and science classes. They inquired as to whether or not I'd be willing to act as a reference for you, which I clarified I would. Basically, they just wanted to know what you were like. I said you were very talented, new to the Math Mania team, and one of my best students. They seemed interested, and I left it at that." Mrs. Gable beamed at Victoria, who was still clutching her acceptance letter. "It seems as though that did the trick."

"Mrs. Gable, I really can't thank you enough,"

said Victoria. "You didn't have to do all that for me. I appreciate it. Probably more than you know."

"It was my pleasure," said Mrs. Gable.

Victoria plopped down into the chair in front of Mrs. Gable's desk, blowing out a long breath.

"I still can't believe it," she said, clutching the letter. "This doesn't feel real."

"It's definitely something to be proud of."

"Now I just have to tell my dad," Victoria said. "But I mean, this is amazing news, right? He can only be happy about this."

"I'm sure it'll be just fine," said Mrs. Gable soothingly, and for a moment, Victoria was on top of the world.

For a couple days, Victoria carried her acceptance letter everywhere she went. It was either in her backpack, or folded in her pocket, or smoothed out in front of her on a table or desk. She couldn't stop looking at it, touching it, and re-reading the words. It was still almost too much to believe. An annoying little voice in her head, though, kept reminding her more and more insistently that she still hadn't told her dad. It was just so nice to have a few days to enjoy the news on her own, to read the letter over and over again, and hold the exciting news close to her chest.

But now, it was time. State finals were only two weeks away, and Victoria couldn't hide her news anymore. Plus, the anticipation was starting to wear on her. It would be easier to just get this over with, and move right to the part where her dad was just excited. She had been doing research, too, on the potential positions for people with engineering or math degrees in the film industry, and the options sounded incredible. Sure, the elite slots for engineers in the industry were few and far between, but it wasn't like Victoria was a novice. She'd always loved the behind-the-scenes aspect of film development and special effects creation, and the idea that she could go to school and eventually earn a degree in that type of engineering was a dream come true. Now, all she had to do was tell her dad.

Victoria held her phone in her hands and flipped it over, then set it on her bed, walked out of the room, and came back to pick it up again.

Just call him, she told herself. *Get it over with, finally. He's going to be just as excited as you are.*

Before she could chicken out again, Victoria tapped her dad's number and took a deep breath as she brought the phone to her ear, trying to ignore the fact that her hand was shaking.

He probably won't answer, she thought as the phone rang. *I'll just have to try again later.*

"Hello? Victoria?"

"Oh, hi Dad," said Victoria, jumping off her bed to pace around her bedroom. "I wasn't sure you'd answer."

"You caught me on my way to a meeting," he replied. "So, I'm free at the moment. How are you, honey?"

"I'm great, Dad," said Victoria. "How are you? How's the trip going?"

"It's going superbly. We're nailing down a lot of important dates for this movie, and negotiating for a few others down the pipeline."

"That's great, Dad," said Victoria, running a hand through her hair. *Okay, it was now or never.* "Look, Dad, I need to tell you something." There was a brief crackling sound, and Victoria frowned at her phone.

"Sorry, Victoria, I lost you there for a second," said her dad. "What was that? You need to tell me something?"

"Yeah, I do. It's, uh—"

"I have something to tell you, too. The date has been set for your reading."

"My reading?"

"Yeah, for the new movie."

"Oh, okay. I mean, that's fine, but what I need to tell you kind of applies to that."

"It's going to be in two weeks, in the afternoon

sometime, so clear your whole schedule for that day."

"Exactly two weeks?"

Victoria's mind was processing the math, wishing she had it wrong.

"Yeah, two weeks exactly. I think you'll love the part—it's like it was written for you. I guess it was, in a way," he said, chuckling. Victoria was fixated on the date.

"Dad, I can't do it in two weeks." Two weeks was the day of state finals.

"Why not?"

"I have a school commitment that day," said Victoria, panic lacing her voice.

"I'll get you out of it," said Richard carelessly, and Victoria heard him say something tersely to the driver in the background.

"I can't get out of it," said Victoria. "It's not that kind of thing."

"Look, whatever it is, we'll rearrange it. I'll call the school if I need to, but you need to be at that reading in Los Angeles that day, and we'll make it happen."

"Dad, I'm not going," snapped Victoria. "Are you listening to me? This thing I have to do, it's something I care about."

"What do you mean? What is it?"

"I tried telling you about it before," said Victoria. "It's a math team, an academic club. We have a really important match that day at a convention center in Anaheim."

"This again? Why are they requiring you to do this to graduate?"

"Dad, they aren't," said Victoria, practically yelling now. "I'm doing it because I want to."

"I don't follow," said Richard. "Honey, this is a very important reading and I need you to be there. I understand you want to honor this, uh, commitment you made, but it's not going to happen. I'm flying back in for the reading, so I'll meet you at the office that day and we'll drive together. That's the end of it."

Victoria was at a loss. *Would he really never understand? Why wouldn't he just listen?*

"I'm not going to be there, Dad," she said. "I'm not going. You'll have to reschedule the reading."

"We both know you'll be there," said Richard, distracted again. "There's no reason not to be. Look, honey, I've got to run. I'll see you in two weeks."

The line went dead. Victoria dropped her phone from her ear, her eyes smarting. Her chest was tight with frustration, her hands still trembling. Victoria wiped a stray tear from her cheek. He wouldn't listen to her. All he cared about was that she was at that reading.

For a moment, Victoria forgot that the whole reason she'd called in the first place was to break the good news about Caltech. She'd been kidding herself. He wouldn't be happy for her. He probably wouldn't even listen to her long enough to hear her announce it. *Has it always been this difficult to talk to my father?* Victoria sighed, sitting down on her bed;

she wasn't sure when she stood up, but now her legs felt shaky and weak.

What was she going to do?

Chapter Fifteen

Victoria didn't discuss the conversation with her father to anyone. At Math Mania practice, she debated bringing it up to Mrs. Gable, but decided against it. There wasn't anything the teacher could do to help her. This was between her and her dad, and they were clearly on very different trajectories. What hurt the most was the fact that he wouldn't listen to her. He didn't seem to understand what she was trying to tell him at all, and Victoria was losing hope that she'd be able to express herself to him clearly. He was expecting her to be at that reading, and she'd promised to be at state finals. If only he weren't so stubborn, maybe she could've gotten him to change the date, but her dad had a head like a rock. And Victoria had inherited that single-mindedness through the blood, she thought wryly.

"Victoria? Did you need something?"

Victoria snapped to attention, realizing that Mrs. Gable had just called the end of a Math Mania meeting and everyone was leaving but her.

"Oh, sorry," said Victoria, standing up from her desk. "No, I'm fine. See you tomorrow."

State finals were in one week, and everyone was starting to get edgy. Victoria was dealing with nerves of her own, complicated by the dilemma she faced. Should she blow off the competition to make it to the reading? It would certainly make her life easier. But even as the thought entered her mind, Victoria dismissed it. There was no way she could let her teammates down like that. It just wasn't an option. Maybe if her dad had heard that she'd gotten into Caltech he'd understand how serious she was about this, but he'd hung up before she could tell him.

Victoria sighed, dropping her books on a secluded table in the library. She rubbed her tired eyes with one hand; when state finals were over, she'd be relieved. The competition would take most of the day, with multiple teams competing at the same time. Teams were ranked, and then eliminated based on their progress throughout the day. Beverly Hills Prep would compete two or three times through the rounds, depending on how well they did, before the final round of the day, which would decide the championship team. Victoria didn't entertain thoughts that they'd have a surprise victory like they had in semifinals—this competition would be the best teams in the state, and Victoria knew their team would be happy just to make it through the first round. She'd watched tapes of the championship matches from past years that Mrs. Gable had shown, and the level of problems was very intense, as were the kids on each team. The competitors were all other private schools, but some were co-ed, so boys competed alongside the girls.

But somehow, Victoria wasn't worried about winning. That wasn't where her energy was focused; more so, she wanted to perform as well as she personally was capable of. It was more about proving something to herself than it was to anyone else. She would do the best she could for herself, and for her team, and whatever the outcome was, she would be satisfied with that. Victoria stayed in the library until it closed for the night, working her way through derivative proofs, and fell asleep with her head on a book until the librarian woke her. As she stumbled to her suite and face-planted onto her cool blue duvet, she just hoped she'd make it to state finals at all.

Just like the day of semifinals, Victoria woke up early on the day of state. She considered the fact that she didn't feel quite as nervous as she had for semifinals a small victory. After showering, Victoria took her time getting dressed, making sure her uniform was crisp and clean, along with her Math Mania blazer. As she dressed, she considered calling her dad. He was probably flying in soon, expecting her to be at a reading she wasn't going to show up to. Victoria bit her lip; she wasn't sure what her dad's reaction would be to that, but she didn't imagine it would be pleasant.

I can deal with him after the competition, Victoria thought. *He'll be mad, but I can't help that. I tried to tell him why I couldn't be there, and he wouldn't listen.*

It was funny to her how easy the decision had been to go with the Math Mania team as she'd planned, and not go to the audition. The reading could be rescheduled, logistically, and the competition couldn't. Plus, she'd made the Math Mania team a commitment that she wouldn't break. She'd be letting the entire team down, and that wasn't an idea Victoria even considered. Maybe at the beginning of the year her choices would have been different, but a lot had changed. And for the most part, they were changes she was proud of, no matter what her dad thought.

Squaring her shoulders, Victoria grabbed her bag, carefully packed with her books and notes so she could study on the bus ride. The day had arrived, and she was ready. As she walked to the lobby to meet Mrs. Gable and her team, Victoria shut off her cell phone. Her dad might freak out, but she didn't care. If he wasn't going to listen to her, she wouldn't listen to him, either.

"Is everyone ready to go?" said Mrs. Gable. "The bus has arrived."

Victoria's stomach flipped, but she nodded, and boarded the bus with everyone else. She was ready.

Victoria flipped through her books and kept her headphones in during the ride, and it flew by. Before she knew it, they'd arrived at the convention center that was hosting the event, and they unloaded from the bus. Victoria wasn't prone to gaping, but for a moment her mouth dropped open as she saw the sea of students heading to the front doors. This was nothing like semifinals—it seemed like there were hundreds of people all converging in the same place.

"Are all these teams here for state?" Victoria asked Mrs. Gable, a little desperately, and the teacher nodded.

"Yes, this is everyone. It looks overwhelming, I know, but the field is thinned very quickly in the first rounds. There are so many matches happening at once that before you know it, half the teams have been eliminated."

"That's not a very comforting thought," muttered Victoria. She'd thought she was over her anxiety when it came to these things, but seeing so many teams made her palms start to sweat. As Math Mania and the rest of the teams filed into the convention center, Victoria saw how large it really was, with annexes and rows of conference rooms where different matches would take place. They were slotted in one of the annexes for their first match. The day would continue through round after round of elimination until the final matches took place in the main room of the hall, with trophies awarded to first through fifth place.

It took a while to complete the check-in process, but soon each girl had been given their badge and been assigned their schedule for the day. Mrs. Gable then led them down the hallway and up the staircase to the second floor, where their first match of the day would be held. Victoria sighed with relief when they were in the much smaller conference room, with a makeshift area for the teams to compete and a judge in the center. When the door closed, it was easier to forget the rest of the teams and just focus on this one match first. The other team was a co-ed school from Sonoma County, and they shook hands as the judge announced the competition would begin in five minutes.

"Now, I want all of you to take a deep breath,

and remember that whatever happens, what matters is that you do your best up there," said Mrs. Gable. "Don't worry about the rest of the teams, or anything else. Just stay focused, stay calm, and you'll all do great."

Victoria nodded. Glancing around at her teammates, she could tell they were nervous, but everyone looked ready to compete. Taking a deep breath as the judge announced the start of the match, Victoria walked to her place with her team members behind her, making sure her calculator, pencil, and graph paper were all where they should be. Before she had a chance to worry about the first question, the bell sounded, and the problem appeared on the projection screen. Victoria bent her head, and got to work.

Chapter Sixteen

By early afternoon, Victoria's right hand was cramping, and her eyes were blurry from studying problems so intently. They'd won their first match by a landslide—as it turned out, the other team just wasn't nearly as prepared as Beverly Hills Prep, and since then they'd narrowly lost the second one. Victoria credited that to one of the girls on the other team who wrote so quickly that Victoria was afraid she might set her graph paper on fire with the friction from her pencil. Now, they were waiting to compete again.

"I'm sorry about that last match, Mrs. Gable," said Victoria, massaging her own hand.

"Oh, don't worry about that," said Mrs. Gable. "We're still slotted to place, if we win the next match."

"Really?"

"Yes—if we win the next one, we'll be competing one more time for fourth or fifth place. If we lose the next match, we're out entirely."

"Fourth or fifth doesn't sound that prestigious," said Victoria, and Mrs. Gable chuckled.

"Maybe not to some of the teams who make it here every year. But for us, it would be an astronomical accomplishment. To place at all is an honor."

Victoria nodded, sipping from her water bottle. She was tired, but feeling refreshed since she'd had a snack. There wasn't much time to feel tired, anyway—the pace of the competition was so quick that by the time you'd finished one match you were thrown into the next one without time to feel your own fatigue. Before she knew it, it was time for the next match, and she took the stage with her teammates in a larger annex.

This match was the most difficult yet—every time Beverly Hills Prep edged ahead, the team from San Diego answered a question correctly, and they were neck and neck again. Finally, Danielle answered the final question correctly, and the team erupted in cheers. Victoria was jumping up and down and hugging everyone she could reach; there was only one match to go, and they just might go home with a trophy.

Victoria tried to focus her mind as they walked to their newest assigned location. The teams competing for fourth and fifth place would compete on one of the larger stages adjacent to the biggest hall. It was a spacious auditorium, with a stage area and benches set up for the contestants. Rubbing her temples, Victoria summoned the last of her energy. She could practically feel how tired her brain was.

This is the last one, she told herself. *The last match*

of the day. Just get through one more of these, and then it's over.

The judge announced the match was commencing, and for the last time, Beverly Hills Prep took the stage. Victoria eyed the girls across from her and her teammates. They looked bright-eyed and calm, and that was intimidating.

Just focus on yourself, Victoria told herself. *Don't worry about the other team.*

Then the first problem was on the projector, and Victoria scribbled furiously, and typed equations on her calculator. The other team answered the first three questions, and Victoria was beginning to panic a little until Angelica answered one correctly for Beverly Hills Prep. After that, Victoria answered one, and the score moved incrementally closer.

As the match progressed, Victoria pushed herself mentally harder than ever before. She answered questions she would've deemed to be impossible to solve even a few months ago. With every single problem that came onto the projector, Victoria challenged herself, and more often than she would've believed, she rose to the occasion. It was exhausting, and exhilarating, and she loved it.

Finally, the last round arrived. Beverly Hills Prep was trailing, and Victoria wiped at her brow as yet another problem was presented to the teams. It was a question about derivative limits, and Victoria couldn't quite recall the process to solve it. Racking her brain, she scribbled on her graph paper—she knew how to do these, but her mind was so tired that she just couldn't quite get there. She couldn't even remember what the score was at this point. The other team answered first, and Victoria shook her head, trying to focus.

Almost there, almost there.

The last question was released, and Victoria's heart leaped. It was a theorem that she recognized, and she typed the necessary elements furiously into her calculator as the seconds ticked by.

Danielle's voice was the first one to call out the answer. All eyes turned their way, and Victoria clutched her pencil in one hand and her calculator in the other. It was the same answer Victoria had written down—she just hoped it was right.

"That is correct," said the judge. "The final score is fourteen to San Diego Oceanview Academy, and thirteen points to Beverly Hills Prep."

Victoria's heart dropped as the other team congratulated each other; she'd been so focused on those last few problems that she hadn't realized that even though she'd answered that last question correctly, they'd still lost the match. To her surprise, Victoria turned as one of her teammates began to congratulate her as well, grinning.

"Awesome job, guys," said Danielle. "Fifth place! I can't believe it. We get a trophy and everything!"

"You're the one who answered that last question correctly," said Victoria, smiling.

"We all helped," Danielle corrected, grinning, and then the whole team was celebrating.

From the audience, Mrs. Gable was clapping wildly; Victoria smiled at her as they shook hands with the opposing team and filed off the stage. As they approached their teacher, she beamed at them, clapping her hands.

"That was spectacular work, all of you," said Mrs. Gable. "Congratulations to each and every one of you. You all worked very hard today, and I'm supremely proud. Now, we'll wait for the final matches to end and then stay through the trophy ceremony to receive our prize, for the first time in the school's history."

As the girls chattered to each other excitedly, Victoria caught sight of a familiar face in the crowd. Turning, she got a good look, and her stomach dropped to her feet. Flanked by his bodyguards, her father glowered at her from the back of the room.

Oh, no. This is really, really not good.

Chapter Seventeen

"Dad?" said Victoria, in shock. She made her way to him through the crowd, legs shaking all over again. She had never seen him look so incredibly angry. By the time she reached him, she was quaking under the ferocity of his gaze. Now she knew how all those secretaries he'd fired had felt.

"Uh, hi Dad," said Victoria. "What are you doing here?"

"When you didn't show up to your reading and weren't answering your cell phone, I called the school. They told me you would be here, at this ridiculous event."

"Dad, I'm sorry I didn't answer my phone," said Victoria. "It's been turned off all day. But this event is not ridiculous. It's something I care about."

"Victoria, why are you wasting your time with something like this? And jeopardizing your future at that, by not attending auditions when you're supposed to?"

"I told you I couldn't make it to the reading," Victoria retorted, her own temper rising. "You just didn't want to listen."

"I didn't seriously believe that you wouldn't come," her dad said through his teeth. "Do you have any idea how embarrassing that was for me, as a professional, for my own daughter to miss such an important meeting?"

"If you'd just listened to me when I said I needed to reschedule it, we wouldn't be in this mess!" Victoria yelled. "I'm a part of this team. I wasn't going to let them down."

"You're a part of this team? This . . . what is it, some sort of math team?"

"It's called Math Mania," said Victoria. "And yes, I am."

"Why? Is this some extra credit thing gone wrong? Why would you involve yourself in something like this?"

"Because I'm really good at it," Victoria answered. "Dad, I know this is going to sound weird, but I love math. I want to be an engineer. I've been helping this team, and the teacher in charge of it, for years. She even helped me get into Caltech."

"You've applied to colleges?"

"Yes. I wasn't sure I wanted to, but Mrs. Gable convinced me to, just in case, and I got in."

For a moment, Victoria thought she saw a surge of pride in her dad's eyes, but it was quickly replaced by anger.

"You should never have done this without consulting me, Victoria," her dad said. "You should've told me."

"I tried to," said Victoria, her eyes filling with tears. "I swear, I tried."

As she wiped at her nose, trying to get ahold of her emotions, Victoria felt a hand on her shoulder.

"I assume you're Victoria's father," said Mrs. Gable, reaching out her other hand to meet Victoria's dad. He scowled at her, ignoring the outstretched hand.

"And who are you?"

"My name is Glenda Gable. I'm Victoria's math teacher, and the coach for the Math Mania team."

"So, you're the woman responsible for my daughter applying to colleges, and participating on teams I didn't approve of?"

"You signed the forms for me to participate," Victoria retorted, "when we had dinner at the restaurant."

"That doesn't mean I approve of this," said her father, and Victoria rolled her eyes. "And I certainly never approved of you applying to colleges without consulting me. Victoria, we have a plan for after you graduate, and it doesn't involve any of this."

"Dad, what if what I want something different now? I don't want to be an actress. I want to be a lighting or sound engineer, or something more along those lines." It was so hard to explain things like this to him. Her dad shook his head. Out of the corner of her eye, Victoria could see her teammates trying not to gape at the scene they were causing, but it was obvious they could hear everything.

"You never said anything like this until this woman influenced you," he said, pointing at Mrs. Gable. "She's coerced you into going against everything that we had planned."

"Dad, that isn't true!"

"Mr. Cambridge, please," said Mrs. Gable. "I can assure you that I only have Victoria's best interests and well-being in mind. I think she's a smart, talented young woman, and I want to see her succeed."

"So do I," said Richard, "and I think I know my own daughter a little better than you do."

"With all due respect, sir, I don't think you're listening to what she's trying to explain to you. A lot has changed since she began helping me in my classroom. And, as you can see, she's an amazing asset to this team."

"She's an asset to anything she sets her mind to," said Richard gruffly, with a touch of pride, "but this isn't right. Long term, it's not what she wants. And Victoria has too much at stake to be wasting her time doing something ridiculous that she's going to realize isn't right for her."

"Dad, please stop talking about me like I'm not standing right here," said Victoria. "I'm telling you, I want to go to Caltech. It's a really good school. I want to pursue a career in the film industry, just the same as always, but in a different avenue. I want to work behind the camera, not in front of it."

For a moment, Victoria thought her dad might understand, but then the moment evaporated. Instead, he glared angrily at her, and then at Mrs. Gable.

"I'll be calling the school about this," he said. "I want to file a formal complaint against you, and remove Victoria from Beverly Hills Prep."

"Dad, are you crazy?"

"Victoria, my mind is made up. I want you to come with me, now, and you'll finish out the year somewhere else."

"I'm not going anywhere," said Victoria. "Dad, please, don't do this. Just take some time and think about it, please. I promise I'm not trying to trick you, and I've been moving in this direction for a long time. This isn't an impulsive decision."

"Fine, stay here," her dad snapped. "I'm calling the school, and the headmistress, tonight. We'll settle this tomorrow, and you're out of there, Victoria. And you," he said, pointing at Mrs. Gable, "are going to be out of a job before you can blink."

With that Richard Cambridge turned on his heel and left the building, parting the crowd as he went.

Chapter Eighteen

Victoria couldn't even enjoy the trophy ceremony because she was so angry with her father. Even by the time they were on the bus on the way back to school, it was like there was a red haze over her vision; her dad might have a temper, but so did she, and she was having trouble controlling it right now. Everyone had stared at her for twenty minutes after he left the convention center because of the scene he'd made. How dare he just stomp in here like that, and yell at Mrs. Gable? Who did he think he was?

He's Richard Cambridge, Victoria acknowledged,

sighing. No one other than her father would have the nerve to interrupt an event this way and demand that she drop out of her school just because she'd missed one audition.

"I'm so sorry about that," Victoria said to Mrs. Gable, who was sitting across the aisle from her with their fifth-place trophy. "That was awful of my dad to act that way."

"Victoria, you don't need to keep apologizing," said Mrs. Gable. "It's alright. This wasn't your fault."

"He's going to complain to Headmistress Chambers," said Victoria. "He always follows through on a threat."

"I can handle it," said Mrs. Gable. "I've dealt with other angry parents before."

"But not my dad," said Victoria, and Mrs. Gable smiled wryly.

"No, not him. Victoria, I don't want this event ruining the day's accomplishment for this team.

Today, we placed in a state competition, and that's huge. Don't let what happened ruin that for you."

Victoria sighed, and nodded. "I know you're right," she admitted. "I'm just so embarrassed. He's so stubborn, and he never listens to me."

"He'll come around," said Mrs. Gable. "You'll see."

The bus pulled in to the Beverly Hills Prep parking lot, and Victoria grabbed her bag and walked down the aisle, exhausted. All in all, this day had been amazing. *Why did my dad have to ruin it for me?*

The hurt she felt was starting to trickle in through the anger. Everything she'd worried about had come true—she'd thought that because she was her dad's only kid, and they had a special bond, that he'd never treat her the way she'd seen him treat his wives. But she was wrong. He'd been mean, and manipulative, and Victoria was more than angry. She was deeply hurt that her dad would act this way toward her, specifically. Maybe that was selfish, or self-centered, but she couldn't help it. He was the only real family she had—what if she lost him?

The other girls were chattering happily, arguing over who got to carry the trophy inside, and Victoria followed along behind. She was glad they were so excited, and she was excited, too. Her dad had even been there to see her competing, at least for a couple minutes. He hadn't even mentioned it, hadn't even acted like any of it mattered. Victoria waved goodbye to her teammates as they parted ways in the foyer. The residence hall was quiet, the other students all either studying or in their rooms. As Victoria walked down the hallway, she was comforted by the familiarity. This had become home in the past four years, and it was especially nice to walk by the paintings and artwork she'd come to know and let her feet guide her. She didn't want to think about where she was going tonight, when her head was still buzzing with everything that had happened today. Victoria sighed, and decided to stop by the dining hall on her way back to her suite. She needed the biggest, most chocolatey milkshake that the reserve chef could whip up.

Victoria slept badly, tossing and turning with vivid dreams. She'd turned her phone back on right before bed and was depressed all over again when the twenty-nine missed calls had popped up from her dad. She hadn't been brave enough to listen to the voicemails. As she lay in the dark, Victoria was swamped with indecision. Was all of this really worth it? Would it have been better if she had just done what her dad told her to do, and stuck with the original plan?

It's too late to think about that now, Victoria thought, turning onto her side. What was done was done. Now she had to live with it.

The next morning, she woke feeling just as tired as she had the day before. Sighing, she dressed in her uniform and headed for the dining hall to get as much espresso into her system as she could before starting the day. Sipping her coffee, Victoria made it to her first class and plunked into her seat.

"You okay, Victoria?" said Annabelle, sliding into the seat across the aisle. "You look exhausted. Are those . . . are those dark circles under your eyes?"

"Thanks for pointing that out, Annabelle," Victoria snapped.

The teacher walked in with an armful of lesson plans and briskly set them down on the desk. Victoria prepared to start taking notes when the teacher spotted her.

"Oh, Miss Cambridge? You need to go see the headmistress immediately. Her orders. Make sure to take your things with you."

Oh, jeez.

The entire classroom started to titter, but Victoria was past caring. She grabbed her stuff and left the classroom, ignoring the stares. Not that she'd ever been one to concern herself with what others thought, for the most part, but in light of recent events, she really didn't think she could care less what the rest of the student body thought of her being summoned to see the headmistress first thing in the morning. Wait a second—her dad wasn't actually here, was he? Victoria wasn't sure he'd ever set foot on campus; they always met elsewhere when he was in the area, and he was a man more likely to be reached by conference call than seen in person. Surely, he wouldn't follow up on that part of his threat from yesterday.

Victoria opened the door to the administrative building and took a left, pausing outside Headmistress Chambers' double doors. Knocking softly, the headmistress asked her to come in, and Victoria twisted the ornate knob.

Her dad was sitting in one of the plush chairs in front of the headmistress's desk—and sitting next to him was Mrs. Gable. Victoria gaped at the scene for a moment, and then walked slowly inside.

"Shut the door behind you, please, Miss Cambridge," said the headmistress.

"What's going on?" said Victoria, closing the door.

"Your father called yesterday and said he had several complaints with the school, and with one of my teachers. I take such things seriously. I've gathered all of us here for a meeting on the subject."

"The subject of what?" Victoria asked, seating herself in the third chair.

"The subject of you," said the headmistress, eyeing Victoria over her silver glasses. Headmistress Chambers sat in her high-backed chair and folded her hands. Today she wore a long velvet dress in deep maroon, and as always, Victoria admitted that the woman looked like a queen.

"This teacher," Victoria's dad said, pointing at Mrs. Gable, "coerced Victoria into changing her entire life trajectory. This is my kid, and all of a sudden she's claiming she wants to be some sort of engineer? She's applied to colleges that I had no idea about. And she hid all this from me."

"Dad, you know that I tried to tell you," said Victoria. "I really did. For a long time I didn't think it was that serious that I was so good at my math classes—once I started focusing on them, I mean. But I love physics, and I've always loved sci-fi and fantasy movies, and I can have a career in special effects with an engineering degree."

"See? See what I'm saying, here?" said her dad, gesturing at Victoria. "I don't know where she got these ideas."

"Mr. Cambridge," said the headmistress, "is it true that Victoria tried to communicate these topics to you, and that you were not receptive?"

"She may have mentioned some of it," said her dad, and as Victoria glared at him he had the grace to look guilty. "I'm very busy, and I don't always get to spend the time with her that I'd like."

"If I may butt in," said Mrs. Gable, "I can assure you that I didn't put any thoughts into your daughter's head. I saw potential, and I encouraged it, but that's all. I would never purposely go against the wishes of a parent."

"Mrs. Gable didn't do anything, Dad," said Victoria, crossing her arms. "I filled out my own college applications, and I decided to join Math Mania. No one forced me. All she did was actually push me not to slack off. And she supported me, which is more than I can say for you right now."

"Victoria," said Richard, looking pained, "I don't want you feeling like I'm not supportive of you."

"That is how I feel, Dad," said Victoria, her eyes filling. "I feel like you don't listen to me. You brush me off when I try to talk to you about stuff. And then you showed up at the competition yesterday, out of nowhere, and you weren't very nice. I told you I got into Caltech, which I'm really excited about, and you acted like it didn't even matter."

Richard leaned forward, his elbows on his knees. He was a man with a powerful presence, and Victoria had only seen him wear anything but a suit once, at a midnight movie showing he'd taken her to when she was about seven and had begged and begged to go. He looked out of place, here, like he was too big for the space.

"Mr. Cambridge," said Mrs. Gable, "I understand this may be jarring for you to hear. I know you had plans for Victoria that didn't necessarily include her attending a four-year college, or pursuing a different career avenue than you'd expected. But your daughter is a talented young woman. I don't want to have caused any sort of rift between the two of you by being her mentor."

"Dad, aren't you proud of me at all?" said Victoria, standing up from her seat. "Hasn't any of this made you even a little proud? You act like you're not affected by anything except whether or not I get a new part in a movie."

"Sweetie, of course I'm proud of you," said her dad. "I'm sorry if that didn't come through, but I'm surprised you even have to ask."

"Yeah, Dad, I do," said Victoria. "I mean,

I'm your kid, but I've seen what has happened in your marriages. What if you got tired of me, too, or decided that because I wasn't doing what you wanted me to do that I just wasn't worth your time anymore?"

"I would never think that," her dad said, looking at Victoria. "Honey, I can't believe you'd even consider that."

Victoria just shrugged, fighting back tears.

"Victoria, you're my only child. You mean the world to me. I just see how talented you are as an actress, and I wanted to push you to pursue that the same way that Mrs. Gable here encouraged you to pursue math, and whatnot."

"The difference appears to be that Miss Cambridge wants to pursue one, and not the other," said the headmistress softly. Richard sighed, then leaned back in his chair, folding his hands across his chest.

"Look, I'm still getting used to all these new ideas. And maybe it wouldn't be such a shock if I was around a little more, but you've always been so independent, and I'm proud of that, too," said Richard, gesturing to Victoria. "I just want what's best for you."

"Me too, Dad," said Victoria. "And maybe we won't always agree on what that looks like, but I need you to listen when I try to talk to you about what I want."

Richard sighed, rubbing the bridge of his nose.

"Well, I guess I'm going to have to get used to the idea of paying for college, then," he said, and Victoria launched herself at him, hugging him tightly.

"Thank you, Dad," she whispered, and Richard kissed her head.

"Don't think you can slack off at Caltech," he said brusquely. "I expect you to succeed at anything you decide to pursue, even if it is something like—what did you say you want to be?"

"Some kind of engineer," said Victoria. "Or something else where I can work behind the scenes with sets. I'm great at physics. I'd probably be a great set designer, too."

"I think I can work with that," her dad sighed.

Chapter Nineteen

"So, Victoria, have you sent in your acceptance yet?" asked Vivi as they sat outside near the arboretum a few weeks later.

"Not yet," said Victoria. "I have a couple more days to officially accept Caltech's offer."

"But you know you want to go," said Annabelle, laughing. "So why are you waiting?"

"I don't know," Victoria sighed. "I know I'm going to accept. It's just fun to prolong the anticipation, I guess. Plus, my dad will be back within cell service reach again, and he wants to be on the phone when I send in my acceptance."

"Where is he this time?"

"Somewhere in Panama now, I think, overseeing production details for a few days," said Victoria. "He said this movie is going to be like a cross between *Indiana Jones* and *Star Wars.*"

"How will that even be possible?" said Sasha.

"I'm not sure, but it sounds cool," said Victoria. "And he's setting up an internship for me with some of his favorite special effects directors, so I'll learn how to do all that cool stuff from the best."

"Okay, you don't need to brag," said Annabelle, and Victoria laughed.

"I'm just excited," she said, tilting her face to the warm sun. And she was. Graduation was around the corner, and that was scary, but also so exciting. There was a whole new part of her life that was about to begin, and all she had to do was reach out and take it.

And I will, Victoria promised herself. It wouldn't be easy, but she knew it would be worth it. For now, though, she'd sit on the grass at Beverly Hills

Prep with her friends, sip her chocolate-strawberry milkshake, and enjoy the sunshine. Her new life could wait just a little longer.

THE END